Advice from a Cat

Daniel Damiano

Other Published Work

Novels
~
The Woman in the Sun Hat
Graphic Nature

Poetry
~
104 Days of the Pandemic
The Concrete Jungle and the Surrounding Areas

Plays
~
Day of the Dog
Plays by Daniel Damiano Vol 1

Praise for ADVICE FROM A CAT (2024)

"What I expected to be a lighthearted, feline-inspired tale turned out to be a deeply introspective and emotionally resonant novel that beautifully explores themes of redemption, loneliness, and unexpected companionship.- If you're a fan of stories that explore the complexities of human nature through unconventional yet deeply meaningful relationships, *Advice from a Cat* is a must-read."
– Kathryn Dare, Manhattan Book Review

"Damiano has written a thought-provoking and emotionally resonant novel that explores how far one person is willing to go to absolve himself. Its nuanced portrayal of human fragility makes it a compelling read for anyone interested in the psychology of redemption and the fine line between selflessness and obsession." *– Sunday's Mail*

Praise for GRAPHIC NATURE (2022)

"*Graphic Nature* tells a compelling story with interesting, believable characters while delivering a nuanced message that's both powerful and important. It also manages to involve the sagacity of life and death, love and loss, the sins of the father, and the indifference of God. You'll want to read it sitting down." *– Sunday's Mail*

Praise for THE WOMAN IN THE SUN HAT (2021)

"While Daniel Damiano could have turned Peggy's tale into one of misery and desperation, he has instead crafted a humorous and uplifting story of perseverance and struggle against the odds." *– Seattle Book Review*
(2021 Beach Read Recommendation)

*To the cats of my present and past:
Chula, Juanito and Dusty*

Special Thanks

I wish to sincerely thank my friends and loved ones who lent their support and provided valuable feedback: Judy Alvarez, Lee Anderson, Cinda Lawrence, and Jack McCleland.

One

As Brian entered the latest application into the Food-on-Feet database, Jeff Gammon spoke dulcetly into his ears: *"And so we come back to the question: What is your best you? Is it you self-gratified? Is it you victorious at the expense of another? Is it you when ignorant to the ills of our world? Or…is it you when giving back? Well, as you ponder that, here's a statistic for you: it has been scientifically proven that the endorphins that course through us when we've simply helped someone in some way is the greatest conceivable high we can achieve as human beings. And so what else can make us feel better, more essential to life and the fabric of our culture, than an act of kindness? And so it would seem to me that the best you is the giving you. The generous you. Not necessarily in any sort of material way, but just in an emotional one. When your sole stake is to do nothing else but benefit another. When that is achieved,…that is your victory."*

"Brian?"

Brian quickly pressed stop on his phone from which his earphones were tethered, "Yep?"

"There's meals on the floor that need to be delivered," grunted Shanda, a fellow case worker, who stood before his desk in her usual posture of indifference.

"How many?"

"Like three carts of hot'n cold. The usual for a Saturday," as she strolled back to her equally small desk adjacent to his, before placing her earbuds into her oversized pocketbook.

"Is Tim here?"

"Nah, he left."

"He left?"

"Yeah."

"I thought we worked until all the deliveries went out on Saturday."

"He said he had to do somethin' for his mother or somethin'."

"Ok. But…people still need to get their food."

"Hey, what can I tell ya'? n'I can't go anywhere myself."

"You can't deliver?"

"I told ya', I hurt my knee. It acts up whenever I'm on my feet for too long. Halfa' these places are four floor walk-ups with no damn elevators."

Brian vaguely recalled Shanda's sporadic limp, but did not want to invest energy questioning its legitimacy. He had to take her word for it, and apparently had little choice since she appeared to have every intention of going home. In truth, Saturdays at Food-on-Feet's base, an office attached to St. Anthony's Community Center in the Bronx, where volunteers once poured in to donate two hours of weekly altruism, were becoming increasingly less popular. And with that, those who were staff, as per company protocol, were supposed to pick up the extra routes, since paid delivery staff only worked during the week. The goal was that there was to be no food remaining, especially since they were closed on Sundays. Tim despised delivering as if it were a trip to the dentist, which made his excuses unsurprising. This week it was his mother. Last week it was a leak in his apartment. At the rate he was going, it was probably only a matter of time before he started using the dead grandmother excuse. It seemed surprising enough that Tim was a case worker and, like Shanda and Brian, was obliged to visit applicants and usually their inquiring offspring to assess if they met the criteria for food delivery. Shanda was more jaded than ineffectual, working as a case worker for about the same amount of years as Tim. She had delivered in the past when necessary, though with ample complaining, and was definitely not a fan of getting stuck talking about the weather with some of the more loquacious recipients. But both seemed to lessen their sense of obligation due to Brian's willingness to take the load. And it did seem like he was the only one who cared more about the housebound clients receiving their food, for they would have few options otherwise.

"Alright, don't worry about it. I'll take 'em all," Brian resigned, his need for penance again overriding his feeling of his colleagues taking advantage.

"Y'sure?" she asked, without any true interest in his assurance.

"Yep, it's fine," as he rose from his small desk from the cramped, fluorescent lit office and walked onto the community center floor where three carts with large temperature-controlled bags waited. He looked at the route lists of all of them, before taking one of the carts into the overcast street. He placed his earphones back in, as Jeff Gammon continued, underscored by the aged cart's ever-present loose and rumbling wheels:

"Your victory is when you give of yourself. When you do something for someone else, be it volunteering at a soup kitchen, be it helping a neighbor, be it a kind word or being a sounding board for a friend who simply needs to speak to someone they believe hears them. When we think beyond our own needs – "

A horn blared, as Brian suddenly noticed he no longer had the right of way while he was midway on the crosswalk, "Sorry, sorry," as he scampered obsequiously across the street with the cart. The car gave another superfluous honk, followed by a *"This ain't the park, douchebag!",* before proceeding on. Brian stood at the corner and watched, remembering that not long ago he might've reacted very differently.

***

He arrived at Gwendolyn Fochetti's apartment on the 4th floor, about 8 blocks from the office. The hallways were indicative of the building's age, matched by flickering lights in need of changing and tan walls dimmed to a corroded brown, all which made the building appear little more than an oversized cavern. A taped sign on her metal door read *"Hard of Hearing – Please Knock Loudly!"* in multi-colored marker, as if scribed by an overzealous child. Brian knew to do so from many previous trips, and at this point knew the exact strength he needed to use so as to avoid jolting her unnecessarily.

"I'll be right there!" she bellowed from a distance.

As this was Brian's most regular route, he also knew to wait about a good two minutes before Ms. Fochetti navigated through her narrow apartment, rendered all the more so by metropolis-like stacks of aged newspapers and magazines, as she made her way to the door. During this time, he'd look down the scantly lit hallways, hear the omnipresent muffled arguments and Latin-based pop music that emanated under the neighboring doors, as if played in a constant loop.

"Coming, coming, coming…" she murmured, through the snaps of unfastening bolt locks, before the door opened. "Yes?"

"Hi, Ms. Fochetti. How are you?" he exclaimed, in a volume that he tried to sustain, but which would always manage to wane.

"Oh, who is that? Is that you, Brian?" her grayed eyes leaned in towards him.

"Yes, it sure is. Good to see you."

"Oh, you too. It's always so nice when you come."

"It's my pleasure."

"It's what?"

He subtly raised his volume, "I said it's my *pleasure*."

"Oh, stop. Why don't you come more?"

"Well, I'm usually on cases or at the office during the week."

"On what?"

"Sorry," he adjusted his volume again, "I'm usually on *cases* during the week. I mainly deliver when we're shorthanded."

"On cases? What kind of cases?" she asked, with genuine intrigue, as if Brian was some sort of private detective.

He'd explained this to her several times in prior visits, but was always happy to reiterate: "Well, it's meeting with people, like yourself, who apply to receive meals. So we go out to meet them."

"Oh, I see. Yes. I remember when I had someone here. Oh, God, that must've been four or five years ago. I forget if it was you. Was it you?"

"No, that wouldn't've been me, Ms. Fochetti. I haven't been doing this that long."

"Oh, alright. And come to think of it, he wasn't nearly as nice as you."

Brian realized that it could very well have been the often begrudged Tim, but didn't want to assume. "Well, I'm sorry to hear that."

"Your what?"

"I said *I'm-sorry-to-hear-that*," he politely enunciated.

"Oh, don't you worry. I'm just glad you're here." She often began her sentences with a requisite *Oh*, as if it made her answers more engaging.

"You doin' okay?" he asked, with a presentational smile.

"Oh, you know. As long as I got my shows, I'm fine. It fills the air."

"Well, that's somethin', right?" he weakly agreed.

"Oh, yes," she concurred, in her usual way. "And I've got the cats."

"That's right," he animatedly agreed.

"And my son'n daughter," she boasted.

"Yes, how nice."

"Oh, yes. And 4 grandkids," she concluded her list, through a grand smile.

"Right, right. How are they?"

"Oh, I'm sure they're well. It'd be even better if I could see them, but, you know, everyone has their own lives."

"Sure. Is your family in the neighborhood?" he asked, having never asked this before.

"No. My son is... Well, I think he's in Florida now. Boca Raton, I think? I can't remember anymore. And my daughter's in New Jersey. Both pretty far away."

"Well, not *that* far," he said, consolingly.

"Well,...far from *me*," her voice suddenly losing its jovial façade.

Brian didn't want to respond too quickly to this. It hit him, as it normally did to see people like Ms. Fochetti; old and alone. Families were often always somewhere but, apparently, never close enough, even if they were within the same city. Rather than continue down this road, Brian at least knew that the food he was bringing was a welcome diversion: "Well, let me tell you what I have today, Ms. Fochetti. I've got one of your favorites: Chicken parmigiana."

"Oh, how nice. With spaghetti?"

He laughed brightly, "Yes, of course, with spaghetti. How can you have chicken parmigiana without spaghetti, right?"

"How lovely."

"And you got a nice side salad. And some butterscotch pudding."

"Some better what?"

"*Butterscotch.*   It's pudding, Ms. Fochetti," he stressed, through a smile.

"Oh, wonderful. Thank you so much, Brian."

"Ms. Fochetti, it's my pleasure. It's *you* I should thank."

"Oh, you stop. For what?," she laughed with playful embarrassment.

"For being so pleasant to talk to."

"Oh, c'mon now," as her hand fanned the air in dismissal.

"No, it's true. Just to speak with good people like yourself. You have no idea."

Not long ago, he wouldn't've paid any mind to someone like Ms. Fochetti or been aware that someone existed in such conditions. It was outside of the narrow world he once resided in, though in hindsight he realized his was not unlike Ms. Fochetti's; rife with mindless diversions, conjoined, at the time, with a dead-end job. Yet through his new vocation, he was now all too aware of how many older people lived in the city, and made it a point to be a positive presence, even if it was ultimately a social distraction of mere moments. But it was because of the brevity of these exchanges that he often thought too much about others' feelings, and wanted his actions and words to satiate, for he knew loneliness would follow after his departure. But saying too much of the right thing could just as easily become excess. Ultimately, he wanted Ms. Fochetti to feel as good as she could for as long as she could feel it.

He looked at her for the moment and, as would happen from time to time, he'd see a mother he barely knew, a grandmother who he knew less so, before coming back to the woman before him whom he wanted to simply make happy, as he brightly shifted: "Now I also have your Sunday meal, which as you know you just need to stick in the microwave for about 12 minutes or in your oven for about 30 at about 325, okay?"

"Okay, thank you."

"It's vegetable stew with some herb mashed potatoes and apple cobbler."

"Apple what, dear?"

"Apple *cobbler*," he said brightly.

"Oh, my weakness," she giggled, as if momentarily 12, while Brian admired the sudden surge of youthfulness. "Now, Brian, if you don't mind..." as she stepped aside, allowing him passage.

"Absolutely. On the counter?"

"Thank you so much. Just watch your step."

"I will," Brian held the meals in his arms as he entered her apartment, so dimly lit that it resembled more of an urban cave, managing to be even darker than the cavernous halls. The familiar smell and dampness all but smacked him in the face upon passing through the doorway, soon after followed by a swift surge into his nasal cavities which would then explode into a geyser-like sneeze, as was his usual re-action to dander and perhaps other mysterious bacteria which resided in the apartment.

"Oh, bless you," Ms. Fochetti said.

"Thank you, Ms….CHOOOOO!", Brian attempted to reply. "Thank you, Ms. Fochetti."

He made his way past stacks of newspapers that looked so old they seemed as crispy as wafers, along-side dust-laden vinyl records and video cassettes. Bits of dry cat food were strewn about, though he never saw the cats, except for the briefest of cameo appear-ances by one of them. It was easy to not see many things that may have been also residing there, but the age and neglect of it were undeniable. To any other delivery person, it was likely sickening. Tim and Shanda would rarely enter apartments when deliver-ing, and certainly wouldn't ever venture into a place like Ms. Fochetti's without aid of a hazmat suit. But Brian felt it cruel to not. He knew no one helped Ms Fochetti - and *that* is what sickened him.

"Right there on the counter, if you'd be so kind, Brian."

Brian entered the kitchen, which was barely distin-guished by the presence of the oven, refrigerator and a large, tilted Garfield clock.

"Right by the sink there's fine," she followed.

If he failed to distinguish the sink clearly enough, he knew from previous visits to simply follow the flies that circulated around the unwashed pots and pans, empty soda bottles and some of Food-on-Feet's trays that had remnants of past meals cemented into them. He placed the trays down and, as if rerun from his many previous deliveries - "RAOW!" screeched one of her cats, on whose tail Brian accidentally (if habitually) placed the meals, leaving him to nearly drop them onto the floor…as the multi-colored feline scurried into the darkness of Ms. Fochetti's lair.

"Oh, don't worry. That's Socrates. You just startled him," she consoled, as if unaware that this pretty much happened every Saturday that Brian came.

"Boy, I never see 'im."

"See what, dear?"

"See *him*. *Socrates*," he emphasized. "He's got a real knack for blending…" as he caught his breath, then "HACHOOOO!"

"Bless you."

"Thank you, Ms…HACHOOO! For blending in."

"Well, he's a tabby, so it's one of his many talents," she smiled. "You can just put them there, Brian. Thank you."

He carefully placed the meals on the counter, which was layered with old magazines on which stood randomly-placed figurines of varying sizes, resembling a strange found-art exhibit.

He was often tempted to stay a bit longer and at least help make the kitchen a bit safer for her, but he still had about thirty more hot & cold meals to deliver. It just wouldn't be fair to the others who needed these meals. Too many people who needed to rely on too few.

"Would you like to have some with me, Brian?"

"Oh, that's kind of you, Ms. Fochetti. Unfortunately, I have a lot of other deliveries," as he quickly wiped his nose. "Would you like me to put the cold meal in the freezer for you?"

"Oh, you can just leave it there. I'll take care of it."

"Are you sure?

"Yes, I have to rearrange some things in there. Are you sure you don't want some chicken parmigiana?"

"That's very generous of you, but I want you to enjoy it all, okay?

"Are you eating, at least?"

While much of their exchange was similar to their previous ones, when new responses or questions would come, Brian could not help but be pleasantly reassured that she was lucid enough to be on her own. The question she would ask about his diet was a first: "Oh, yeah. Of course. Don't you worry about me."

"Well, I just want to make sure you're okay. Because if you're okay, then I know you'll be back." She smiled, as did he. He was moved, again, to the point that he almost forgot his allergies, before she grabbed his hand and shoved several balled-up dollar bills into it. "Now this is for you, and I won't hear – "

"Oh, no, Ms. Fochetti, I really can't."

"Brian – "

"No, you never have to give me anything. It's my pleasure to be here. You should know that," as he gingerly placed the money back into her tiny, frail hand.

He smiled at her, before she touched his face, as had become her tradition – her near blindness a valid excuse, as if the bristles of his afternoon shadow were braille: "Such a good young man you are."

Two

—

Brian sat in the fifth row pew, alongside the usual ambient infant caterwauls which always seemed to prevent a Sunday service from being truly meditative, but the words of Father Devon more-or-less managed to cut through, mellifluously aided by his slight Irish lilt:

"From Isaiah 58:10," he then read: "*And if you give yourself to the hungry, and satisfy the desire of the afflicted, then your light will rise in darkness, and your gloom will become like midday.*"

He took a moment to let this sink in to his parishioners but, in these moments, Brian wanted to believe that such quotes were for him, more so than most. He could absorb every second of a service under the belief that mass was more of an ongoing spiritual conversation meant to remind him that he was on the right path.

"We live in a time of great division. If we give just minutes of our day to what is posted on news scrolls, it's all but inescapable, isn't it. At least it seems so.

And such exposure, however minimal it may be, can often lead us to the belief that this is our world. This is what we are a part of. Right? We are a part of the division because, perhaps, we believe we are better than others. Perhaps, we are a part of the adversity that seems to prevent our peace of mind. All the negatives are there for us to pick from the cyber stems like toxic fruit. One can even say that these are all the apples that've come from the same tree that Adam once picked from. So what does that tell us?"

Several dutifully murmured, "That we're all sinners."

Father Devon heard this, smiled, "Well, we don't necessarily have to say that action makes us a sinner, for we are all that anyway, yes?"

Brian nodded, as did others.

"But what it really tells us is that we're becoming part of a growing problem in our society. Yes, everyone seems to do this, right? We're on the subway, the bus, we're on our phones, and most aren't exactly reading excerpts from Isaiah."

Some knowing laughter matched the father's smile.

"What they're reading can be toxic, quite often. It doesn't make them or us sinners by that action, but what it does is make us contributors to our state of crisis. The very things we complain about to our friends and family. Division. It is there. And it comes in myriad ways. From misinformation. It comes from a sort of gratification in the misfortunes of others, even though we may not dare voice this. But our role in this world is to love. It is to be empathetic and aware that there is always someone who has it worse than us. No one had it worse than our Lord, and yet he wouldn't alter his actions in any way because he cared more for others than himself."

Another gentle breeze swept through the church from the nods of agreement, as Brian felt the draft, then smiled.

Brian was draped in the dim light of the confessional booth, still always unnerved by the words that emanated through the screen, after he uttered the requisite, "Forgive me, Father, for I have sinned. It's been one week since my last confession."

"Please tell me your sins," Father Devon gently offered.

"Well, I feel I..." he struggled to find the right phrasing. "Well, Father, um…I feel I was judgmental, or have been acting a bit judgmental in some…instances."

"Judgmental."

"Yeah. Um… Yes, I'd say so."

"What have you done that you feel makes this a sin?"

"Um…well, I just… I mean, I haven't really voiced anything to anyone. I guess…sometimes I just question other people's… Like people I work with. I feel that their heart may not always be in the right place."

"So you've been critical of this?"

"Yes, but not…not outwardly. Just to myself. But I try not to really dwell on it. I just… I enjoy what I do, and try to move on from it."

"These are co-workers?"

"Yes, that's right."

"And so you feel they aren't giving of themselves perhaps to the extent that you are?"

"Well, I…yeah, I suppose so. And I think that I'm probably being unfair. And I guess that's why I feel it's a sin."

"You feel that it's a sin to judge them."

"Well, that *is* a sin, isn't it? Isn't that… *Judge not lest* – ?"

"Well, that's more of a judgement call, no pun intended. But perhaps if you do feel that there is an imbalance in your work environment, it may be beneficial to voice it diplomatically."

"Really?"

"Sure. Why not? It doesn't mean that you're right, of course, but if you feel this strongly enough, then perhaps mentioning it respectfully to your co-workers can help alleviate certain things you're feeling."

"That's, yes, that's… I've wanted to but… I guess I didn't want to offend anyone or make them feel…"

"That's understandable. And you don't have to say anything, of course. But it's an option that you have, and perhaps in so doing it, there will be greater balance among you and your co-workers."

"That's… I appreciate that, Father. I do. But… I guess I feel like it's audacious of me."

"Why do you feel that?"

Brian took a moment, knowing he was anonymous to Father Devon, but nevertheless felt shameful in revealing too much. For him, it was never something he could reveal in any depth, but broach in as vague a method as possible: "I just… Well, not long ago, I wasn't…I wasn't a very good…person."

Father Devon waited for more. "Well, that's a little vague. In what way?"

Brian was frightened of the mere question, as if having already divulged too much, before taking a breath enough to add nuance to the ambiguity: "I…I suppose I just didn't understand what was important. I lived for myself and for nothing else, to be honest. And I'm not that way anymore. But I think back to the way I was, and…I guess I see it in some of these people who I work with, so it's…it's hard to be critical of them."

"And yet it seems like you've learned from how you were to become the person you are, right?"

"Well, I'd like to think so, but…maybe not."

"Well, it doesn't mean that you have less of a standing to convey your feelings to your colleagues. Perhaps your experience in being how you *were* has informed you all the more to be able to help them."

Brian nodded, "I…I see." This wasn't the first time he heard such advice. It also derived from the *I Ching*, as well as Jeff Gammon's audiobook that he listened to with regularity; how the experience of one can only help someone who might not have the same level of experience. The essence of growth. One can be the seed as well as the root as well as the flower.

Father Devon continued, "Remember what today's sermon covered, if that helps you. We should all seek to be a part of the solution, not the problem. Right?"

"Right."

"So what do you think, based on your relationship with these people, is for the greater good?"

Brian nodded again, convinced that the actions he would take the next morning would be assuredly just.

Three

—

"What?" Tim snapped.

"I just… Don't take offense, Tim. I'm just pointing out something that I've been seeing," Brian said, in as low a register as he could make audible.

"Look, I bust my ass here, okay?"

"Well,…"

"I mean, if you choose to work extra hours for no pay and do deliveries'n shit, that's on you, but it doesn't mean I'm not doin' my job, dude."

"Okay, Tim, but us doing deliveries when we don't have enough volunteers is a part of our job, right?"

"And I've done them, Brian."

"Yeah, but not always," he managed, gingerly.

"Dude, I had to help my mother on Saturday, okay? I told Shanda."

"Okay, but…Shanda's not your manager."

"And neither are you."

"I know that."

"Well, Ismet isn't here on Saturdays, so who else should I've told? The cafeteria staff doesn't give a crap."

Brian felt clearly that he wasn't making any strides in bringing this up with Tim. Tim was not him, after all. He knew he couldn't impose his work ethic on someone who clearly had developed contempt for his work. He did the bare minimum, and it was getting less so. Ismet may or may not have known the degree to which Tim was slacking but, ultimately, Brian knew that this exchange was having quite the adverse effect.

"Okay, Tim. That's cool. Just forget we had this exchange, okay?"

"Forget? First thing on a Monday, I haven't even had my coffee, and you want me to jus' forget this?"

"Yeah, just forget it. I'm sorry," as he attempted to go back to his desk…

"Yeah, I bet. I think I'm gonna' tell Ismet."

Brian stopped. "Tell Ismet what?"

"That you tried calling me out like this. Throwing me under the bus."

"Tim, I'm not throwing you under anything. I haven't even said anything to Ismet," Brian replied, under a whisper.

"Yeah, right."

"Tim, I haven't. If I said something to her, would I be speaking to you directly?"

"I dunno', man. You're strange."

Brian scrunched his face, "Strange?"

"Yeah, man. You love this too much. You think you're Mother Teresa. Jus' pull back, dude."

"What do you mean *'pull back'*? Care less?" Brian was even more surprised than Tim that this came out.

Tim looked at Brian sharply. Brian wasn't sure what Tim was capable of when being challenged like this, though it wasn't his intent to corner him. Brian went to the office hoping beyond hope that Tim would get it. He prayed for it that morning. Meditated on it. Read excerpts from the *I Ching*, even. He recalled his confessional exchange with Father Devon, which empowered him to approach Tim discreetly. And, of course, while in transit, he listened to Jeff Gammon's excerpt on being proactive in dealing with adversity. But to look into Tim's dagger-plunging eyes, it appeared all for naught.

Tim continued to stare at Brian, "Dude, I think we're done here, okay?" as he punched his hand into a paper bag and retrieved a grease-laden bacon, egg and cheese sandwich, which he gruffly placed on his desk. "Jesus fuckin' Christ," he murmured under his breath, before turning his hostile attention to his computer screen.

Brian walked away, passing by Shanda at her desk. Despite the pulsating volume of music that spewed from her earbuds, she likely gathered Tim's hostility and would no doubt be on his side, once apprised of the details.

***

That afternoon, Ismet called Brian into her small, cramped office.

"If you feel you have something to report about a co-worker, it's best to bring it to my attention, Brian. Okay?"

"I understand. I'm sorry, Ismet. I thought it'd actually work out better for me to address this with him and not…you know, draw attention."

"It's not the best way to do it, in this instance. He took issue with your tone and that's why we're here."

"Well, I didn't have a particular tone. I wasn't talking down to him or anything."

"I'm only going by the information that was reported to me, Brian. We're a small staff here so it's just best to do what we can to avoid confrontation. We're all working very hard."

Brian internally disagreed with this, but simply nodded, unsurprised that Tim would go this route.

"And there's something else we need to go over, okay?"

"Um, sure. What…?"

Ismet pulled some of Brian's past applications, "Now part of why we're having shortages of volunteers can be manyfold, okay? I'm aware of this. I think a lot of it is just the times we live in now, post-pandemic. And I appreciate you being quick to pick up the slack with weekend deliveries. Believe me, I'm aware that you're doing more than most on this, and I really appreciate it."

"Sure."

"But…what will help curb the amount of deliveries is being more objective with who qualifies. Now I have some of your applications from the last few months and, based on our new members, see that pretty much all of yours you've approved."

"Okay."

Ismet looked at Brian with concern on this. "Like *all* of them."

"Okay. Is that…not good?"

"Well, you're aware that these people can't just get these deliveries. They have to pass a certain criteria, which is why you guys are sent out."

"I understand."

"And in all your cases, almost without exception, Brian, you're approving them for delivery. And based on experiences with some of our volunteers and with some staff, not all of them appear to qualify."

"Well,…how would they come to this?"

"Brian, I've had more than a few reports of deliveries coming back because these people aren't home."

"Really?"

"Yes, really."

"Are they sure?"

"Brian, you know that if they knock and no one's home they have to report it to us. If they're dead in the apartment, that's one thing. But these are cases of them going out for walks. And if they can go out for walks, they can go to the store and get food for themselves."

"Well, sometimes they go to doctors appointments, right?"

"Right, but not in most of these cases. My point is that I think you're a little too quick to approve these people."

"Well, it's only because I think they're entitled. I mean, Ismet, with all due respect…"

"Brian, I get it. They're old, they're limited in many respects, we all see our grandparents in them, but we can't cover these rapidly growing numbers. We don't have the budget. We don't have the manpower. We don't have the volunteers. You don't want to stay late on Saturdays having to do all these additional routes."

"If I have to…"

"Brian, it's not feasible. And if some of these people aren't home, it's even less so. We're wasting pay, we're wasting food."

"But I'm trying to save us money. I don't even report the hours I deliver."

"That still doesn't make it acceptable, Brian. Now I need you to use better judgment with these cases, okay?"

Brian sat there a moment as if struggling to find an alternative or expand on his defense, but ultimately could only nod.

Four

On the subway home, with a bag of a freshly nuked Food-on-Feet meal upon his lap, he mused over the events of the day. It was a *"day of challenges"*, as Jeff Gammon would refer to it. A day in which the good energy he wanted to emit was thwarted by others to who that energy meant little. With Tim, it was clearly ego. He could never have someone like Brian give him even the impression that he was deficient in his work ethic, even if he clearly was. Why he remained with the organization was a puzzle to Brian, though he understood it likely came from addiction to a certain routine. Addictions to adverse behavior or practices or loathsome jobs were not uncommon in American society, as Brian had learned from all the TedTalks, self-help and spiritual books and masses he attended. In Tim, he even saw his old, jaded self, which made it all the more challenging in dealing with him.

As for Ismet, while Brian felt that her intentions were good, he also felt that she had become submerged in an allegiance to a bureaucratic machine; budget and numbers, which trumped the higher purposes that no doubt inspired the inception of an organization like Food-on-Feet. It was not averse to what Brian thought of politicians: They come into their roles with all the childhood aspirations of being a channel for good before eventually the reality of political compromise engulfs them. But he chose this route, which he thought would be immune to such requirements, and that is what distressed him. He was not a wide-eyed young man out of high school or college, undaunted as to the possibilities for corruption. He was 38 now, and came into this new vocation by way of wanting to make a change and help people in need. He wasn't a jaded civil servant, nor was he someone who had failed at other professions and this was all he could manage, by default. In retrospect, he felt that his prior ambitions were actually too low for failure to even be a possibility.

For years he had worked as a security guard, and had watched the world go by for much of that time as he stood beside a revolving door. His world was one of blind observation. Working at high-end buildings which usually housed financial companies rumored to have unfathomable fiscal girth, he spent his days observing the immaculate suits and dresses and shoes and moussed hair that traipsed by him en route to an elevator, wherein these people no doubt spent much of their existence discussing profits, and all for profits' sake. He realized one day that it was too easy to do what he was doing. It was too easy to pretty much sleep standing up like a Clydesdale in a suit, collect work hours like worthless sea shells, then go home and sleep lying down, with his only off time spent having mindless conversations over too many drinks with one or two friends living the exact type of ne'er do well life. A life of contentment. A life of habit. His years increasing. His weight increasing. It was a *useless* life, he'd come to discover. It was being part of the problem, as many of the sources of his daily teachings would say. To be aware only of what would get him to the next day, and the only intrigue being purely diversions: the next episode of a streaming series, music videos on YouTube, ball games, video games, etc.

But after hearing of Leslie Scanlon's passing, after several weeks in which she was in a coma, he soon realized that he needed to cleanse everything. Sage the room, so to speak. It was then that he came upon a local commercial for Food-on-Feet, which he had seen ad nauseum over the years, but usually served as his cue to go to the bathroom or mute the TV and play a round of *Squash the Mailman* on his phone. But one day, it struck him. He had begun volunteering at Food-on-Feet on Saturdays, donated groceries to local pantries, gave blood, stopped eating meat and drinking alcohol… Within weeks, he was committing so much time to volunteering and charities that he had burned through his vacation and personal days. When he decided to quit security and become a case worker at Food-on-Feet at half the pay, it felt as if his old life had all but been eclipsed by a new one, which was exactly what he wanted. The time spent with his friends now seemed wasteful to the extent that it pained him to see them. So much was dispensable about how he'd been living. Things became particularly frayed with his then-girlfriend Sara, who was unable to process the sudden change in him. The growing caveat between them came to the surface on a Valentine's Day evening, during a disastrous dinner out that Sara initiated. It was also the same month that Leslie Scanlon's ex-husband would begin his 5-year sentence. At this point, Brian was all but consumed by altruistic compulsions, which would monopolize what little dialogue was transpiring between them…

"You know, he won a Purple Heart in the Korean War? He's fascinating. And he has a daughter who's Korean. He adopted her after the war. She's a civil rights lawyer. He put her through law school. I mean, what a wonderful man."

"And this is…"

"Jack Tolbert. One of our meal recipients. I thought I mentioned that."

"Well, you're telling me a lot of things, Brian – "

"He's a meal recipient," he repeated, as his eyes darted just about everywhere but towards her, "I approved him for deliveries about three weeks ago. Lives by himself. Had three strokes. His daughter lives on the west coast, so he doesn't have any family near. Just homecare nurses."

"Well, that's nice that you can – " she barely managed…

"I mean, that's what great about this organization, y'know? I mean, these people would starve. And it's barely thanks to federal money. It's mainly private donations. People give so that others can eat. So that's why Food-on-Feet exists. It's necessity. I mean, it's literally preventing starvation of thousands of housebound people."

"I know, Brian. You've mentioned it."

This response finally made him pause. "I'm sorry. I didn't know I was repeating myself," as he finally noticed his long untouched eggplant marsala before him, before seeing a homeless man pass by their outdoor café table: "Sir?!" he called out.

"Brian, not again – "

"Sir, would you like something to eat?"

Sara could only lower her head, as the other surrounding patrons observed an exceptionally filthy man stop and emit his multi-faceted urine scent throughout the exterior dining area… Brian quickly if sloppily wrapped his eggplant and sauteed carrots in several napkins, before seeing that it would not work for transport.

"Brian, just let the man go, please. This is – "

"Excuse me? Waitress?!" he called, summoning a soon-to-be repulsed and dumfounded waitress to their table. "Could you please bring a to-go container for this? And some plasticware? Thank you."

The waitress looked at the homeless man, gauging that he was why Brian was requesting this, before awkwardly heading back to the kitchen.

At this point, Sara was more embarrassed than anything, as Brian attempted to engage with the man draped in what looked like a raincoat over several well-soiled ponchos on an unseasonably warm February evening, "It'll just be a minute and we'll get this right off to you, okay?"

The man smiled awkwardly, revealing two or three teeth that more accurately resembled burnt corn niblets.

"You live nearby, sir?"

"Brian,…" Sara hushed…

"Sara, please. You live nearby?"

The man nodded, and it was at this point that Brian felt English may not have been the man's first language. "One moment, okay?" as he held up an animated finger, before getting up to find the waitress with the take-out container, leaving Sara to sit before the man, as she looked at her plate, nearly paralyzed. While it likely took about 30 seconds, it felt like 5 minutes before Brian eagerly returned with the container, which he then spooned the entirety of his dinner into,

"Here ya' go."

The man nodded again, and gave another burnt corn smile. As he started to slog away, "Oh, sir! Bread?!" Brian called out to him.

"Brian, for Godsakes…"

"Here ya' go," as Brian handed him several breadsticks from their basket. Again, the man nodded, smiled, before walking away at a pace akin to a walrus ambling across a beach. His scent now having drowned out the once omnipresent smells of parmesan and basil.

With the eyes of all the couples at the neighboring tables on them, Brian sat down, a tear in his eye and barely a smile. It was then that Sara slowly lifted her head to address him.

"Brian, you can't just do that, okay?"

He paused, clearly perplexed. "Why can't I?"

She looked at him, so clearly baffled, then whispered, "Brian, what's wrong with you?"

He scrunched his face, "Nothing's wrong. Why do you ask that?"

She took a moment, then a breath. "I'm just not understanding this."

"What's to understand? I just gave him some food."

"You gave him your entrée. You gave another your salad. I mean, why did I even take us out? We may as well've gone to the park and fed the homeless there."

"Sara, what's the matter with you?"

"What's the matter with *me*? I wanted to take us out on this special day."

"Every day can be special, Sara. You don't need some commercial holiday to make it special."

"Well, it's special to *me*, okay? And we haven't really seen each other of late so I thought this would be a nice occasion to re-connect a little, y'know? And you're making everything about where you're working and all the nice things you do, which is great except that you're making speeches and drawing attention to us."

"No, I'm not."

"Yes, you clearly are. Look around. We're like unwanted entertainment here tonight."

"Alright, so fine."

"And you have no problem with that?"

"Problem with what?"

"Brian,..." Sara needed to reshape her words when speaking to him now. It was like she was learning a new language on the fly and couldn't keep up. "Brian, what happened to you?"

He took a moment, taken aback by her question. "You keep asking that, and I've told you nothing. I'm just... I've tried to explain this to you, and you don't seem to want to understand."

"Understand what, Brian? One day you started in with all these self-help things.   All this inner-self stuff. All of a sudden we never see each other, and when we do, like tonight, you're like a public-service announcement."

"I don't know what you mean."

"I *mean* we can't have a conversation."

"We can converse. I just may not want to discuss the things we used to talk about."

"And my question is *why*? We connected on some level before, didn't we? I mean we were together for two years. What were we doing?"

He made it a point to absorb this and carefully consider her question, and without a trace of defensiveness, "To be honest, Sara, I don't know what we were doing."

She sat with this, and it was as if she could see the end coming. "What do you mean?"

Again, he paused, and as gently as possible "What were we really talking about before I started volunteering and changed jobs? I mean, really. What, Sara?"

She took this in, but unlike Brian, couldn't help but be offended. "We talked like a normal couple, I thought."

"Well, what's that to you? I'm not being sarcastic. I'm really asking. Going out on Valentine's Day because it's 'Valentine's Day' and not because of any other substantial reason?"

"This day means something to me."

"But why?"

"*Why?*"

"Sara, this day doesn't have anything special about it except a reason for people to buy candy and cards. You think that guy cares?"

"Who?"

"Him," he whispered, gesturing to the distance.

"What, the homeless man?"

"Yes."

"Are you serious?"

"Every day is the same for him. Either it's bad or it's a little better, and if I can help make it a little better, what's wrong with that?"

Sara didn't want to be too quick in her responses, for she was aware that Brian had an unusual defense; his generosity of spirit. But it was the suddenness of it that baffled her, as it was now as if his soul had been snatched by a stranger. She took a breath, what seemed to be one of many, then emitted a snicker that she could no longer restrain: "You know what's ironic here? That just last summer I wanted us to go to that yoga retreat upstate, right? You barely could indulge me to go. And when you got there, what'd you do half the time. You played stupid video games on your phone and checked baseball scores. I mean, here we were at this retreat where we're supposed to be all zen'n everything, and it meant nothing to you."

"That was then, Sara, okay? I'm embarrassed about that."

She was surprised by this. "Okay." She didn't quite know how to follow up on his admittance of poor behavior.

"But, with all due respect, Sara,…maybe you should ask why you just gave up on it yourself."

In his question, it was impossible for her to hide resentment, likely in that it was tethered to her own inability to find spiritual balance. "Because I thought those people were phony. And it wasn't making me feel better, okay? My parents were making my life hell, and I was looking for stuff, and that wasn't it. I agreed with you saying it was bullshit."

"But I was wrong, okay? And I'm saying that I've learned that we can't just… At least *I* can't just live for easy gratification, Sara. Life's…life's about something deeper and if I want to explore this and donate my time to these things, that shouldn't offend you."

"It offends me that you think you're better than everyone you used to associate with because you suddenly took this enlightened turn."

"I don't think I'm…" He took a moment to absorb this, and attempted to give proper texture to what Sara was observing, as he looked down at his plate, and everywhere else but at her: "Sara, look, I've lived a…a pretty inactive life up 'til now, and not everyone gets to see it before it's too late. I'm lucky I'm not dying or too old to make a difference, so I'm just taking some action. That's all. We all make choices, and that's…that's my choice. And yours is yours. And if you don't like it, or can't understand it, then…" He paused, then realized he needed to close with looking at her. And in his look, he could not theorize but assure her of one thing: "Sara, I appreciate this dinner and I know it meant…something to you, but I think it's obvious that we're not…we're not really connected anymore."

And while it seemed obvious at this point, his reply nevertheless struck her. She still thought that he would allow their relationship to linger, despite their growing differences. But his observation all but confirmed he was someone else now. She swallowed. "Right. Well, I guess that makes sense. Yeah, maybe I'm one a' those transitional girlfriends, right?" as she tossed her cloth napkin onto her barely touched plate. "The one you dated before you marry a born-again Christian or something."

"Sara – "

"Like Lucas, right? He's your friend for like, what, 10 years, n'now you can't be bothered with 'im."

"You don't have to bring that up."

"Well, it's true, isn't it?"

"That's my choice."

"And it's your choice because why?"

"You're creating an argument here. Okay?" he hushed. "I'm just trying to live a better life. There's nothing wrong with that, but there *was* something wrong with how I…" He stopped.

"How you what?"

He paused. "Sara,...I saw...", he couldn't bear to finish the sentence.

Sara waited, clueless as to where he was going. "You saw...what, Brian?"

As he looked at her, he became certain that he would not admit to anything, except to say, "Sara, I'm ashamed of who I was...and I need to get as far away from that as I can. And that's as much as I can tell you."

Sara continued to look at him. It was clear that for all the clarity Brian was attempting to provide as to the insubstantiality of their relationship, it was perhaps more habit than logic that kept her there, needing more words to transition out of a two-year investment. After an unbearable few moments, Brian resumed, if awkwardly but with as much honesty as he could summon without details: "Sara, I just... One day, I just looked at my life and realized I wasn't doing anything. I wasn't helping. I was just watching. Watching at my job, complaining about stuff. All these things that I wasn't taking any responsibility for. It's like I was just lying on the beach and just watching an ocean and having no control over anything. Everything was just a big wave, and everyone was swimming this way and that, and I was just observing and complaining about it all. I just... I mean, I'm happy to show you some stuff I've been reading – "

"No. No, Brian – "

"Sara, I've been reading *The Benevolent You* by Jeff Gammon. He's fascinating and really inspiring –"

"Brian, please," she barely restrained. She let out a sigh, as if to ease out of her hostility, which then dovetailed into her own regretful admittance. "I think you said it best. We're probably not meant for each other anymore. I mean, it's not like you were ever gonna' propose or anything. That mighta' been our end, except it probably wouldn'ta' been for another year, when I started getting impatient. So maybe you saved us time."

She sat there with her eyes moistening and looked at Brian, who had no words for this – mainly because he agreed. He only felt bad that it seemed, for the first time, that she really needed him. But he knew they could no longer coexist, particularly with what she would keep reminding him of. Women looked different to him now, due to what he had seen just a few months prior - and the fatal result of it.

He was ultimately glad that when they parted that night, she never called again. It just made things easier.

***

After departing his train station in Queens, he would take the less convenient route that would circumvent the now infamous 79th Street between 35th and 36th

Avenue, while carrying the still warm pot pie and mashed potatoes left over from Food-on-Feet. He approached the corner on which a man he had come to know as Jakween had established his card-boarded residence. On some days, he would be awake and active in organizing his life's inventory, which was scattered around him, consisting of blankets, cans, bottles, and a few items that would be of little use to him as someone who lived outdoors: a coffee pot, a toaster, a Magic Bullett blender, etc, which Brian had deduced he likely found and would eventually sell. In that mode, he would always be welcoming of Brian, as if he were the jovial proprietor of a general store that no one frequented. On other days, he'd either be out and about the neighborhood, or asleep, as he was this time. Brian placed the tray along with plasticware somewhat within his enclave so that it was relatively obscured from outsiders' visibility, warmed by imagining Jakween's smile once he discovered it.

As he entered his apartment building three blocks away, he saw Chad Seleski in the lobby coming out as Brian was entering. The rush of good feeling at leaving food for the affable Jakween would be quickly replaced by unsettlement at seeing Chad. They were never overly familiar, but had certainly been neighborly at one time. But now it was awkward for Brian to see him. So much so that Brian had considered moving, which was further justified since the lesser pay he was now making had made living there by himself much more challenging. Chad caught his eye, "Hey", he said under his breath, in a tone that at least made it easy to not commit beyond it.

"Hey," Brian barely replied, as he quickly walked past him to the wall of mailboxes. He unlocked his box, slowing his pace once seeing that Chad had exited into the street. He looked at the door, took a breath, then pulled out his mail before heading to the elevator.

While his one-bedroom apartment was the same residence he inhabited for the last 12 years, it had more recently become rife with self-help and spiritual books and DVDs, replacing the presence of his favorite horror movies, games and more erotic fare, which had long been banished. Lying on his musty couch, he read his favorite excerpt from the *I Ching*, "The Li Hexagram", which focused on avoiding the superficiality of life and how, as one ages, it is of primary importance to find the center, what is truly essential, and avoid superfluous issues in the periphery. He carried this with him and often read this passage when in transit, as he listened to Jeff Gammon or any in a number of people who had become his inspirational teachers. He'd gravitated most to Gammon, and had even once attended a speaking engagement in midtown, which served also as promotion for his latest book, *The Benevolent You,* which Brian had read voraciously before eventually purchasing the audiobook. Brian continued to play certain sections of it, which often underscored his workday, helping also to tune out Shanda's unrelentingly pulsating techno playlist.

Gammon was the former Founder and CEO of a multi-million dollar tech company for almost 20 years, and claimed to have one day simply walked away from it all and donated a majority of his wealth to charities. The very act of his giving, in his words, is what awakened him to his true calling – that of encouraging others, of any walk of life, to do the same. It wasn't as much about donating money as time. He preached that a giving world was the cure for most ills of the world. When one gives, one's altruism, when connected to the feeling of appreciation from the recipient, creates a spark that can help ignite positivity in the atmosphere. Brian hadn't necessarily seen such results in his fellow staff at Food-on-Feet, but saw evidence of this in the meal recipients, like Ms. Fochetti, and when he would serve food at local shelters. And even on the charity walks he indulged in with growing regularity, especially now that summer was here. The next Sunday, he was to be one of thousands participating in the *Legs Against Lupus 5K Walkathon.* It would be his 5th charity walk in the last two months. He had accumulated more miles in the last year than in the entirety of his life prior.

He certainly didn't have much fiscal freedom judging from his relatively svelte bank account, but his personal account was filled with gratification for all that he was doing to create a better world. He felt at least that he was part of the solution now.

Five

—

By the time he made it past the 3-mile mark, Brian felt a surge within him. For someone who either stood in place or sat on his couch for much of his prior existence, being on the threshold of yet another completed charity event was immensely satisfying, as was the energy he absorbed from his fellow walkers who strode with the same level of gratification. It was easier now for Brian to be immersed in such an ocean of benevolence, but at times he found himself looking at an individual, often a white man of similar age, and wondered if they'd always been this way; if the compulsion to do a charity walk or run or cycling event was another extension of what they gave of themselves on a regular basis – or was it merely sporadic symbolism. Was it like many who only volunteered at Food-on-Feet once in a blue moon, or those who ladled soup at shelters only on Thanksgiving, as if solely to make God aware that they were worthy of Heaven? Had they had a prior life of gluttony or sloth or passivity, and was what they were doing now designed to make up for their past? *Everyone has their own story*, as Jeff Gammon noted. *And our stories aren't just our past. They're the entirety of our lives. Not just what we fall into but what we become through our own efforts. But the only thing that really matters is what your story is*, he followed. Whenever Brian's toe dipped into the pond of remorse, he would reiterate this in his mind, like one of many mantras he taped to his refrigerator at home and on his computer at work. His story wasn't over. It was still being written. That is what mattered.

He crossed the finish line, then, amidst cheers from both participants and ambient well-wishers, he heard "Congrats!"

He lifted his head from his craned position to see that this was directed at him, as she stood before him somewhat out of breath but smiling. "Oh, me?" he asked.

"Yes, of course. 5 kilometers is no slouch," she followed. A not unattractive young African-American woman, within Brian's age range, who had just removed her *Legs Against Lupus* shirt to reveal a much looser-fitting one that read: *Life is Like a Box – It's All About What You Put Inside*, fittingly within what appeared to be – a box. Her build was somewhat husky, but by no means heavy-set, while her hair was best described as lively – curly and bouncy, that may have made her appear a bit younger than she was and accented her vibrance.

"Oh, well. You, too. Congrats."

"This is the longest one I've done since last summer."

"Yeah, me too," as he stretched his legs before finding a bench.

"Have you done this one before?"

He was somewhat surprised that she apparently thought to sustain a conversation. "Uh, yeah. I did it last year, too."

"Easier or harder?"

"You mean, comparing this year to last?"

"Yeah. For me, they tend to get easier 'cause you get more conditioned."

"Yeah, I agree," he smiled weakly. "Yeah, I think once you get it under your belt, it's no biggy."

"Sure."

"And, hey, it's only walking, right?"

"Right," she laughed, a bit too grandly, then coughed. Then coughed again. Then coughed again.

"Are you okay…?

"Oh, yeah. All good," she straightened herself up, as if sensing that no more coughs would follow, before she sipped from her water bottle, which appeared to reignite her: "Oh my God, the first time I did the cystic fibrosis one, it just about killed me."

"Oh, yeah. I did that last year."

"Did you?"

"Yeah."

"The first time I did it, about three years ago, I don't think I walked the same for like a week after," she laughed. "I'm doing the *Ride To Stop Domestic Abuse* soon. You?"

He hesitated. "Uh, yeah, I think so."

"Cool. Maybe I'll see you there."

"Uh, yeah. I… Maybe. I have to…make sure I'm registered." He sat and bent his legs on a nearby bench. He definitely knew he was registered for it, and even donated $800 with a nearly maxed credit card, but something within him did not want to reveal any specifics to this stranger.

As gregarious as she seemed, she was aware enough in Brian's tepid answer to note that he may have wanted to be unto himself, and it was that awareness that at least alluded to Brian that she wasn't imbalanced. "Okay, well,…get some rest."

He weakly smiled, "You too, thanks."

She walked away – and that appeared to be that. He never gave much thought anymore to a woman's potential interest in him. He never assumed it and, further, didn't seek it. Not anymore. It had been over a year since he and Sara split and, be it in a conscious or unconscious way, felt that another attachment at this stage of his life to be an encumbrance. More accurately, it was something that he simply couldn't face.

But as he soon saw her congratulating others in the distance, he felt embarrassed at even thinking that she had other intentions or that he was, in any way, an exception.

***

He sat at the end of Arnold Fechner's small dining table, with his questionnaire before him. Mr. Fechner sat alongside his increasingly stressed son, Darren.

"So Mr. Fechner, you're normally by yourself here?"

"Yes, I am," he grunted.

"Do you go out by yourself?"

"Yes, I – "

"He doesn't," Darren interjected.

"Yes, I do," Mr. Fechner insisted.

"Dad, you don't go out," Darren delicately uttered, obviously attempting to avoid inciting him or embarrassing himself in front of Brian.

"I go out!" Mr. Fechner slammed his scaley fist onto the dining table.

"Dad, you know you don't. And just saying you do is gonna' prevent you from getting meals."

"What meals?"

"Meals from this gentleman's organization."

"Who the hell is he, anyway?!"

Brian weakly smiled at this, having assessed individuals with memory issues before. It had been repeated to Mr. Fechner several times within the last 30 minutes why Brian had been there, but it didn't seem to be registering. "Mr. Fechner, I'm with Food-on-Feet."

"Food on *what*?"

"Feet, sir."

"*Whose* feet?"

"Well, the people who deliver food's feet."

"Food to who?"

"To anyone who's eligible."

"Eligible for what?!"

"Dad, just listen to him. He's trying to explain," Darren interjected, through a sigh.

Brian then attempted, "Well, it's mainly designed so that we can bring free meals to people, usually older people, who fit the requirements."

"You see, dad?" Darren added.

"See what?"

"They deliver food right to your door. You don't have to cook dinner. They bring it to you. But if you tell them you go out all the time, they won't give them to you."

"I don't need 'em."

"Of course you need them. What're you gonna' eat?"

"I cook for myself."

"He doesn't cook for himself," Darren whispered to Brian.

"Yes, I do. I can hear you!"

"You don't cook for yourself, dad. You have toast."

"That's cooking."

"That's not cooking. It's toasting. And you can't just have toast. You need nutrients. And me or Vickie can't come here every day."

Mr. Fechner sulked and stewed. It was clearly humiliating for him, but this wasn't unusual. Brian had also seen this before; the dichotomy of the aged parent who felt demeaned by needing such a service alongside their son or daughter who were trying to sell their feebleness to lighten their load of responsibility. It was understandable, certainly. But Brian now had Ismet's admonishment in his ears. All of a sudden, someone he clearly would want to have this service might now be rejected based on Food-on-Feet's fiscal constraints.

"Okay, well, let me ask you this. Mr. Fechner, are you usually home within the range of 11am to about 3pm."

"Who knows?"

"Yes!" interjected Darren.

"I may be here. I may be out," Mr. Fechner barked.

"Jesus Christ..." his son sighed.

"I have my own life! You're sayin' I gotta' keep myself chained to the radiator just so I can receive these Goddamn meals?!"

"Dad, you're not understanding this, okay? We have to make sure you're eating. Vickie and I aren't nearby. We can't come here every day and make sure you're taking care of yourself."

"What makes you think I'm not takin' care of myself. I'm doin' jus' fine."

"How're you fine? All you have in the fridge is spoiled macaroni salad and a half a' box of Baking Soda from 2002."

"You don't know what the hell you're talkin' about," Mr. Fechner grunted, before getting up and heading to the living room where he proceeded to watch the blasting local news.

"Dad, please…" Darren gave up, then turned to Brian, "Look, sir. I'm sorry, is it Brian?"

"Yes."

"What can we do here so that he gets these meals? I don't know what else to do. He's by himself. We live in Long Island now."

"Well, the thing is that we can only deliver to the predominately housebound. If they're not here, we have no place to leave the food, and so if that's going to be an issue…"

"It won't be. He'll be here. He thinks he walks everywhere. It's old memories."

It could've been true. Or the son may've been so desperate, he was lying about his father's daily rituals. Brian had also seen this; the exasperation of the off-spring. Those who were truly flummoxed by the process by which their parent or parents demanded their independence at the expense of what services could be offered to them.

He sensed that Mr. Fechner might not be a fit for the Food-on-Feet delivery program but, once again, could not bring himself to reject the application.

***

One night a week, Brian also volunteered at a suicide hotline. Much of his night shift consisted of biding his time with reading or listening to Jeff Gammon's audio book before a call would come in, which appeared to narrow the distractions of the world down to a grain of sand.   Very often it was a younger individual, which provided an interesting counterbalance to his days dealing with older people with varying degrees of impairment. The only common denominator would usually be loneliness or some sort of isolation. Most times, one call would take up the majority of his shift, as it was important to defer the call duration to the caller.   Aside from this being more evidence of his being part of a societal solution, it also served to broaden his listening skills to the point that seemed as if he had learned another language. In his old life, he would mindlessly rattle off his complaints of humanity's failings; attitudes from building residents where he worked; his disgust at their sense of superiority purely on the basis of their financial status. When he knocked back several Heinekens with Lucas, it always appeared to be the same script; complaints with no remote solutions or willingness to ponder them, with the end result leaving him bloated and content that all of his diatribes were justified.

Now he was to be a large ear with a selective tongue. He had to be the one to assure the caller that he was there for them. He was not judging them. They were not wrong, but perhaps only looking at things from a limited perspective. He also needed to restrain the urge to spout mantras. He understood that everyone was different. The response that one receives might not necessarily work the same way for another. Human beings were varied, and he now knew this. He knew that all were flawed. No one of the earth was immune to being weak or vulnerable. He also now knew the power of simply being present for another who was struggling in some way.

"I just don't see what all this is anymore," Robert revealed. His voice not dissimilar to others Brian had spoken to. Soft and insular.

"What do you mean, exactly?"

"I don't… It's like I look at things now and it just doesn't seem real to me. It's like I see how the earth is like… I don't know, like a way station. Like it's just a test, y'know? Like it's not about living, it's about enduring. Does that make sense?"

Brian understood what Robert meant. At times, he felt that himself, though he never considered himself to be suicidal. But the brevity of existence on earth was something he could not help but address in the new incarnation of his life. He witnessed it in the food recipients; how so many appeared beyond the twilight of their lives, and were basically in a holding pattern until God summoned them. And yet, what appeared to drive Brian was the belief that, while one is of the earth, they deserve a life of dignity and joy and safety, if at all possible. And so it seemed that things he was doing, both in his day job and in his volunteering, was often designed to keep physical and mental impairments of others at bay, at least momentarily: What a nice meal could do for someone sitting in their apartment alone. What listening and identification could do for someone seeking understanding, even amidst a world that did often seem to be a test of endurance.

"I understand. You're not alone in thinking that, Robert," he responded, his voice soft.

"Have *you* felt that?" Robert asked.

He considered. "Yes, I have."

"Doesn't it suck? I mean, there's assholes who're making a living off creating all this fucking conflict and stuff, and it's like everyone's eating it up."

"Yeah, but not everyone."

"It doesn't seem that way."

"Well, listen, I sometimes feel that way, too. Like everyone is falling in line with that kind of attitude, but then…I walk outside and see people doing good things. People who're on the right side of things, y'know? And then I know that what I'm seeing in the news or whatever isn't the whole truth."

"I don't see it."

He took a beat. "Do you socialize with anyone, Robert?"

"Not really."

"Do you have friends or family who you see or can talk to – ?"

"No. My family's fucked. I'm gay and my parents think I'm basically possessed by the devil," he couldn't help but laugh at this.

Brian had heard this before, as well. It was almost the template for young suicides. Young individuals ostracized from their family for one reason or another, but also being socially incapable of maintaining healthy friendships, which often left them without a healthy sounding board. And so they often found themselves down the rabbit hole of the cyber world, leaving them exposed to the worst news in a matter of a few keystrokes. He looked down at his copy of the *I Ching*, and asked Robert if he had heard of it. He hadn't. It was then that Brian felt compelled to recite a passage entitled "The Li Hexagram". He hadn't done this before, and tried to recall if, in his training, reciting from a publication was frowned upon. But he went with his instinct and read the following:

"The many little frills surrounding a situation confuse you. Look for the central theme. The source. The

seed idea. And the solution is easier. Be reasonable. As you grow older, you see that life is very fragile. This causes depression. Do not over-react to cure the sadness. To do so is unnatural, not the real you. And as you grow older, you will see that human nature is vain. This may cause cynicism. Reexamine and re-dedicate yourself to your motives and values. The lesson here is not to be misled by the myriad parts of a problem, but rather to seek out its central theme, its source, its seed idea – and avoid extremes and excess."

Brian then waited.

Robert seemed to take it in. "How old is that?" he asked.

Brian thought, then "Thousands of years, I think."

"Wow," he pondered. Then a moment, in which even his breathing could not be heard.

"Are you there?" Brian asked, with a sudden con-cern.

"I'm here," he responded, as if still absorbing.

"Do you have…any questions about what I just read?"

"When did you start reading that?"

"The book? Uh, gee, over a year ago."

Robert took a moment, as if still pondering the words. "Did someone tell you about it?"

"Well,…it's kinda' funny. I'd heard about it for years and used to just make fun of the title," he weakly laughed, only because it was true. "I mean, I didn't have a clue what it was, aside from something originating in China. But then, one day, I watched an interview of someone, a sort of motivational speaker, and he mentioned how it was one of the books that he carries with him and keeps him sorta' centered. And…I guess, at that point in my life, I felt I needed centering. So I got it and started to read it and carry it around with me."

"And it helped?"

"Yeah, it did. I mean, it wasn't the only thing. But it was certainly something that helped."

Robert sat with this, as Brian carefully allowed space for him to do so. "Why did you need it?"

Brian paused. "Why?"

"Yeah. I mean, was it just where you were at? Did something happen?"

Brian hadn't really been asked about his turning point by anyone since Sara, especially since he had receded from the people of his past life who would be the most likely to question the change in him. There was his father and younger sister Kim, both of whom he was distant from, but still in touch with. He'd usually see them at Christmas, but he had elected to volunteer the last two. But they were so removed from his life, especially the one he now lived, that he felt it didn't much matter what he did, for they didn't seem to particularly care. But with Robert, a veritable stranger, he suddenly found himself vulnerable. His dilemma was that he wanted to be forthcoming with a young man obviously clinging badly enough to life to call, but he couldn't possibly go into details. It was beyond a phone call. And worse, it was a place he found unbearable to revisit.

"Um…to be honest, Robert, it was just a low place for me. I'd lost my job. I'd broken up…with my girl-friend. I was…struggling with finances. I didn't have a real relationship with my family. I was, well, just…in a bad place." These were not the reasons, but he felt these fabrications would work well enough, for at least he knew that these were the reasons that many others had hit their own bottom, even previous callers who he now felt somewhat guilty in borrowing from. "I guess I'm saying that you're not alone. And in read-ing something like the *I Ching*, it made me realize that, yeah, the world is full a' crap sometimes. Some real distractions that take us off track. But…you know, we can block it out and focus on what's important."

There was silence again, and in that silence, Brian could almost hear Robert musing. Just like he would be eager to console Ms. Fochetti and distract her from her own solitude and sense of abandonment, he felt the same compulsion here – but this was a young man on the verge, out of his vision. He could only be sparing in his imposed wisdom, but needed to remind himself to be first and foremost an outlet.

"Hm," Robert managed.

"Does that make sense to you, Robert?"

"Yeah," he answered. "I get it," he followed. As he continued to think, followed by an exhale, "Wow."

They would speak about that passage for the better part of the next hour, appearing to suppress Robert's depression. Something he never knew existed was placed in front of him, and Brian could not help but smile at this young man's suddenly boundless curiosity. By the time their call came to a close, Robert had already ordered a copy online and asked if Brian would be there the following week to discuss this more. Brian happily said that he would.

Six

—

Late Friday afternoon at the Food-on-Feet office, Brian was entering one of his remaining applications into the database. Jeff Gammon barely managed to drown out Shanda's throbbing dance music and Tim's seemingly ongoing conversation with a usually unknown friend through his bluetooth, as he alternated between keystrokes and sips of an omnipresent Mountain Dew. Usually Brian managed to be unto himself for most of an afternoon in which they were at the office at the same time. While it was preferred, it nevertheless bothered him that he felt so removed from Shanda and Tim. However, he realized some time ago that his commitment to his job was on a different plain, and that his idealization of his role was more resented than respected. It was now all too clear that while this may have been somewhat of a career to them, it was more of a career barely upgraded from a survival job. He knew that unless Ismet dropped dead and one of them somehow inherited the position by egregious default, these jobs were not much different to them than his last job felt to him. They were bodies obligated to sit at their desks and enter data when they weren't bodies in the field laboriously interviewing potential meal recipients.   Further compounding these feelings was the radio silence from Tim, since Brian had attempted to enlighten him as to the fact that the weight being pulled was not quite equal among the three of them. Shanda seemed to side with Tim passively, which was predictable enough, as she bore some blame for her own apathy. She would still speak with Brian regarding work-related matters, but her prior if fleeting efforts at engaging with him regarding anything else had all but dwindled.

As far as Brian was concerned, while it would certainly make the climate in the office more pleasant to have at least some mildly congenial repartee with the only other people he was crammed into a dimly lit office with, it ultimately did not impede his production. And it gave him more time during the day to reenforce Jeff Gammon's altruistic philosophies:

"We all know the expression 'There but for the Grace of God go I'. But what does that mean - really? When you see someone ill, dying from cancer or afflicted by Parkinson's disease, it is often the one quote from the Bible that we seem to know. In short, 'I'm glad it's not me'. But 'There but for the Grace of God' means something specific. It is saying that all but a stiff breeze may be sparing us from such afflictions. We're

not chosen to be healthy over someone else. We're simply, at the moment, fortunate to not have what is often the object of our sympathies. But in a day, things can change. My father was healthy; playing racquet-ball, hiking in the hills, whitewater-rafting, ...and the next day he was befallen by a massive stroke. He was virtually paralyzed for the next 12 months before he died. A man in the prime of his life. It can happen to us. And so we must never lose sight of what we have, what we can give and what we can contribute to the world's greater good – especially while we have our health. Because things change. Just like you can change."

By the time the chapter ended, Brian shifted his head from his screen to see that both Tim and Shanda had left for the day. It was an interesting note to end the day on, since Gammon mentioned his father; a di-chotomy to the relationship Brian had with his own. His father was still alive and lived upstate in the same town where he had lived the entirety of his life thus far; living in the dusk of a fairly uneventful existence. He'd remarried several years ago, long after Brian's mother had passed, but the marriage didn't work out and now his father lived alone in the house that Brian and his sister Kim were raised in in Crawberry, New York. His mother's passing seemed to dull any real allegiance Brian had to family. Though he was 13 when she died, she was alive long enough for him to remember her characteristics, some of which he couldn't fully appreciate at the time. He recalled that when she wasn't working as a secretary at a local realtor's office, she often spent Saturdays teaching Arts & Crafts for free to pre-schoolers from low-income families in a neighboring town. Brian even resented the time she spent doing it, feeling abandoned at the lack of time she came to spend with family, but ultimately he would come to realize that she was giving herself to those who had less than he did – at least that was the optimist's side of it. The other side, as he also suspected was equally possible, was that she would sooner spend her weekends with unfortunate strangers than with her own husband, thus reinforcing a marriage that seemed to be so obviously loveless. In hindsight, Brian had become more like his mother, at least the altruistic aspect, after living much of his existence like his father, who never seemed to enjoy his work as a retail manager. Who was overworked and so often too fatigued to smile. Not particularly supportive. Not particularly…anything. The one real distinction of his behavior that Brian recalled from his youth was when his father purchased a handgun after their house had been broken into one day. Brian's mother objected to the purchase which, quite possibly, contributed to the growing chasm between them. It was of little surprise that it was still present in the house, residing on the top shelf of his father's closet. Brian's new phase didn't prompt him to reach out any more than he did before, especially as his father seemed to be a mirror of Brian's former self; a mirror which he could not look at for very long without cringing.

***

"Tank you, my man," exclaimed Jakween, standing alongside his cardboard home, as he received another freshly nuked meal that Brian brought from Food-on-Feet's kitchen.

"My pleasure, Jakween. Hope you like it."

"I always do, man. Always. How was yaw day, my friend?"

Brian always smiled when Jakween asked this. He could barely fathom someone living in a box on a sidewalk having the capacity to even consider how someone else's day was, and yet Jakween always managed to happily inquire and seemed to genuinely care, as if his domestic status was a choice.

"Oh, it was fine, Jakween. But it's always a little better when I see you."

"C'mon, man. You don't have to say dat," Jakween laughed, which only seemed to exaggerate his Jamaican accent.

"I know I don't, but it's true. I wouldn't lie to ya'."

"You sure you're not jerkin' my chicken?" he added, with an even broader guffaw, especially when he managed to incorporate a Jamaican-tinged innu-endo.

Brian could only laugh, "You should do stand-up, my friend."

"You know, friends tell me dat for years."

"You should. You're a hoot."

"For years, dey say *'Jakween, do one of dose…dose open microphones. You funny as shit'.*"

"Absolutely."

"I don't know. Dass hard, you know? And then a lota' comedians, man, dey unhappy, you know?"

"Well, yeah, that's…"

"You hear about dem. Dey make everyone laugh, den dey go home and cry into deir pillow or dey drink or dey do drugs."

"Well, some of them, yeah…"

"Iss hard business."

"Well, you could be an exception, maybe."

Jakween smiled, "We'll see, my friend."

With his meal in his grip, and in his smile, Brian could sense that this would never be a real pursuit, nor did Brian truly believe it would be - and shortly after, even felt silly in making the suggestion. However, he couldn't help but be impressed that a man who lived in a box by a vacant pharmacy could actually make a successful stand-up comic's life seem unenviable by comparison. Still, Brian always felt obligated to shed optimism on what was clearly a less than desirable liv-ing situation. He often found himself walking that line of wanting to help too much, but understood by now that he could not impose his desires for someone. Their ambitions or lack of them were something that only they could initiate, and their delusions were their right. Food was at least something that omitted judgement. Everyone needed sustenance to live whatever kind of life they were living, be it by choice or circumstances that might not ever be known.

He made it through the lobby and elevator ride to his apartment without seeing Chad. It was always hit-or-miss, no matter when Brian got home, which often put a slight twinge in his stomach upon his every entrance into the building. What little he knew of Chad was that he worked more than one job, and he wasn't sure if anything had changed in recent months. The only other thing he knew about him was that he was married to a woman whose name had vacated his memory, and he had a young daughter who must've now been around 5 or 6. He had seen them so rarely, he was fairly certain that his face had little distinction for them. But Chad's presence continued to unsettle him. Every time he headed up to his apartment, he wondered if it'd be wise to move. He could barely afford the apartment with the sole wage he was incurring, and Chad, who even though resided on a floor above him, still served as a recurring reminder of something he was living every day to suppress. Further, his job wasn't even a convenient commute, with him living in Queens and the office in the Bronx. The logistics of why he should leave were all around him, and yet something was keeping him there.

On Saturday morning, he clasped his coffee as he gazed down at the children's playground across the street from his building; usually something he would do as a meditative start to his Saturday, even though he'd be going into the office soon. He would take in an overcast rainy day just as he would a sunny day adorned with the bluest of skies, like this day. He had come to appreciate all phases of meteorological behavior, having instilled in himself that one's mood or optimism for life should never be at the mercy of weather. This was a philosophy obtained through one of many self-help books and podcasts he'd inhaled over the last year or so, but particularly from Jeff Gammon. However, he had certainly come to appreciate the activity of the playground when the weather permitted. The sounds of the kids in the distance would often feel as soothing as a flowing stream for him, giving him a strange comfort that life was happening, and it was filled with possibility. The children who occupied the playground he felt were green as to the ills of the world, and he wanted them to embrace their ignorance. It was like an innocent painting that came to life in the same way; the same sounds. The same color shirts and shorts. The same man, roughly in his 50s, who would be sitting on a bench within the playground, wearing the same brown fedora, with a book in hand.

By mid-afternoon, Brian had come out to the floor wherein the carts were always distributed. Many of the deliveries had been completed, but there were more than a few remaining due to the reliable shortage of volunteers. This would be the first time in the last three weeks in which Tim stayed to deliver, no doubt in response to his discreet departures of the last couple of Saturdays being brought to the surface. Yet his laziness would still come through, as he grabbed the closest route to the office so as to lessen his footsteps, leaving Brian to take the remaining two furthest away from the office. Shanda had been out the entire day, claiming her daughter was sick, which may or may not have been true.

But, of course, he would always take his favorite route, even though it was the farthest away. He would again deliver to Ms. Fochetti, who would express her deep appreciation for Brian's arrival, as always. And as he often did, Brian would bring her weekend hot and cold meals into her darkened lair, placing them on the kitchen counter upon which were the unaltered layers of knickknacks and newspapers. Her sink had the additional remnants of recent meal trays, as well as older ones. The same few flies circulated, as if regular tenants. And again, he managed to accidentally place the meals upon Socrates' tail, before the cat again faded into the darkness. Only this time, Brian noticed something about him, after releasing another climactic sneeze: "Is it me or does Socrates have three legs?" he asked with a smile, before wiping his nose.

"Oh, he certainly does. Since I got 'im," she announced, with a certain pride. "And y'know what? I always say, if he doesn't complain, why should I?" she smiled, incurring a laugh from Brian.

"Well, that's a good philosophy."

"A good what, dear?"

"A good *philosophy*."

"Oh, yes. And that's why I named him Socrates," she smiled.

"Well, that's pretty fitting, I'd say."

She nodded, "Isn't it, though? You know where I found 'im?"

"Where?"

"In the garbage!" she exclaimed, still appalled all these years later.

"You're kidding."

"I'd heard these meows for a few days every time I would drop my garbage down the shoot, until one day I was walking in the lobby near where the trash comes down, and heard it even louder. I went in, and there he was. No one had gone in there for days. He was filthy, thin as a toothpick, he had some sort of goop on him from all the trash. I took him home, cleaned 'im off. My God, it took me at least three hours to get everything off him, he was so embedded with stuff. Oh, it was awful. And would ya' believe, it wasn't until after I cleaned him off that I even noticed he only had three legs? It was as if that was the least of what he'd experienced. And, well, he's been with me ever since. Bless 'is heart. I don't know what I'd do if… Well, anyway. That's the story."

"Huh. That's, wow… That's some story."

"Oh, you're just humoring me, but thank you for listening."

"No, I'm not. That's a very nice story. I'm not a cat person myself, but that's still a very – "

"Why aren't you?" she asked, with more surprise than judgment.

"Oh, just… It's nothing against them. I'm just allergic."

"You're what?"

"*Allergic*", he enunciated.

"Oh, I see."

"Yeah, I've always been. I know it's a lame excuse…"

"No, it's not. That makes sense, too, considering how you sneeze when you're here. My kids are the same way. At least that's what they tell me. And yet you still come and you're so nice."

He regretted even revealing his allergies, even though they should've been obvious to her by now. Even more, he regretted that it made her recall her children and the excuse that they possibly used for their absence. He still didn't want to judge them. He didn't know them, after all. Judgment, especially considering his past, was not easy for him.

On his way out, he risked overstepping as he stood in her doorway: "Ms. Fochetti, if you ever need help with anything in your apartment, I can give you my personal number."

"You can give what, dear?"

He slightly raised his voice, and spoke slowly, as if it were the most important thing he had thus far said to her: "I can give you my personal number if you ever want help with anything in your apartment."

"Thank you, Brian, that's very sweet of you. I'd love to have you over for dinner, whenever you'd like."

"Oh, that's…that's very kind of you, Ms. Fochetti, but I meant if you needed any help with…,like, taking some things out for you. You know, giving you a little more space," he elaborately smiled.

She paused, as if confused by this. "Space?"

"Yeah. Just so…y'know, it'd be easier for you and the cats to get around," he replied, delicately.

"You mean remodel the apartment?" she asked innocently.

He could not help but chuckle at this, then enunciated, "No, I'm afraid I don't have that kind of talent. I just mean…take some of the stacks of papers out. Just to give you more room in here."

"You mean throw them away?"

"Well, uh, yeah. I mean…"

"Oh, no. No, no, Brian. I'm fine. These are very important. But thank you."

"You sure?"

"Oh, yes. Yes, yes. I never know when I need to refer to something. There's some important things in here," as she touched a nearby stack, as if protecting a child.

He looked at the nearest stacks, saw clothing and furniture catalogues from years ago, and knew that there could be nothing of real importance in any of her piled surroundings, unless she had an urgent need to research the price of ladies' slacks from a decade ago. But, again, he did not want to impose his own concerns. He knew that she was unto herself, with little contact with her offspring. He didn't know their feelings for her, or what kind of mother she was, but at times found it hard to suppress his contempt for their seeming neglect. And then again, he thought of when his father would become enfeebled and having to contend with making sure that he was cared for, especially since his sister Kim might not want to grab those reins; her relationship with their father not much closer, and with her own family in Connecticut a viable excuse

"I understand, Ms. Fochetti. But, please, if you need something…"

"That's very sweet, Brian. Hold on. Let me just…" as she ambled awkwardly towards him, she once again tried to force him to take a balled-up handful of bills…

"Ms. Fochetti, please, you never have to do that. For me or for anyone who delivers, okay?"

"Oh, I don't offer this to the others, Brian. Just you."

"Well, thank you, Ms. Fochetti, but please, I really can't accept it. Not now, not ever," he said softly, and with a smile. He was sure she would offer again. It would *all* happen again, despite the new things that would occasionally pop up. And nothing would stop her from admiring him in the moment; his kindness, his youth. She then touched his cheek, another of her usual compulsions, and looked at him with her nearly blind eyes, "Such a good young man you are."

***

He sat on the subway home and overheard it. It was the rare occasion that his ears weren't plugged up with the voice of Jeff Gammon, as if subconsciously hoping he would never hear such an exchange. Two black middle-aged utility workers sitting behind him, apparently exhausted from their day which likely began before dawn, who nevertheless could not contain their indignance:

"You wana' talk about no justice, this guys gettin' out after a year'n a half."

"A year'n a half?"

"Yeah. Kills his wife in broad daylight. Dozens a' witnesses. n'he's gettin' out."

"'cause they say, what, it was crime of…what, crime of…?"

"Crime of passion, right. It wasn't *intended* or whatever. Said he had roid-rage or some BS. But he fuckin' killed her."

"How long was the sentence?"

"S'pposed t'be five years."

"Five years?"

"'n'he's gettin' out in 18 months. You know why?"

"He white."

"Well, that don't hurt, but here's the *ultimate* reason."

"What?"

"His father's a judge."

"In New York?"

"Yeah, big shot circuit court-motherfucka'. It's right here," the man referred to his phone.

"They said that's why?"

"No, they ain't *sayin'* it, but you know that's why."

"It's who y'know or who doinked ya' mother."

"Fuckin' shit, yeah. Man, I remember when this shit happened. This was like two blocks from me."

"You saw it?"

"Naw, man, it was all done when I got there. Worked a fuckin' 15 hour shift that day too, after an electrical fire downtown. I'll never forget. Came home, the whole block was filled with cops. Paramedics'd already taken the lady to the hospital. All too late."

Those last words rendered Brian momentarily deaf. He knew who they were talking about, even amidst the bevy of crimes that had taken place in the city's recent history. It almost seemed fated that he hear this, and yet he could not have been less welcoming of such news. The crime was the sole reason why he'd come to largely avoid any media coverage, and found out about most things by accident. He'd long gotten rid of his plasma screen, cancelled his cable, and did his best to "tune out the noise of the world", which, as Father Devon noted, was often the cause of so much societal stress and dissension. For the last year and a half, Brian had felt well served by his blissful ignorance, like the children in the playground except with a taint that could only come from adulthood. He cared only about what he could contribute to the world, the difference he could make to an individual to the extent that his financial struggles appeared less daunting than they would have in his prior life. But now he heard those words like a horrifying echo, *"All too late"*, as he looked at his phone, and did a search for the name he still knew like the most dreaded of memories: *Randy Scanlon.*

Seven

He pulled up the first search from a local city publication, and read the following:

A former Jackson Heights, Queens resident who was convicted of the brutal beating and ultimate death of his ex-wife, Leslie Scanlon, will be paroled next month after serving just 18 months at Branding Correctional Facility in upstate New York. Randy Scanlon, 42, was sentenced to 5 years for his ex-wife's death. A crime that was relegated to a manslaughter conviction due to the nature of the crime being, as Scanlon's defense had proclaimed, a crime of passion and one likely enhanced by the assailant's use of steroids, at the time. This defense succeeded despite Scanlon already having prior police warnings culminating in a restraining order, which was in effect at the time of the incident. The crime was of particular note for having at least a dozen bystanders witnessing the ultimately fatal beating, none of whom interceded, though several did give detailed accounts of what transpired once law enforcement had arrived on the scene.

He stood on the crowded platform after exiting the train, and felt that feeling in his gut. It was what he usually felt upon entering his lobby when in fear of seeing Chad, except it was magnified to what felt like infinity. In an instant, all that he took pride in, his work, his volunteering, his compulsion to help, was eviscerated by such news. He fruitlessly thought if he hadn't sat near those two utility workers, he would never know this. It was why he no longer watched the news or read papers or made efforts to look up things online. It was expressly a design to avoid finding out what he had just heard. Now he had this unfortunate knowledge and it would set him into a near trance.

He navigated his way home without conscious awareness of his movements or the walk signs at the end of the crosswalks. Even in his distracted state, he avoided the infamous block. He made it through the lobby and up to his apartment with remarkable fluidity, before he realized that still within his hands was a warm leftover meal he had brought for Jakween; "Shit," he cursed under his breath. It was all he could do to make it home, exhausted and distressed, but the thought of Jakween not having this meal to enjoy still managed to usurp everything else.

The elevator arrived on the fourth floor and, as it opened, to his shock, there was Chad, alone. Brian could barely grasp the irony that he would see him now, especially when he had just managed to avoid him prior. He held the meal in his hand, as Chad looked up from his phone to see him. Brian wanted to run back into his apartment, but knew just as quickly how odd that would seem. How could he continue to live in this building with Chad just one floor above, especially after fleeing upon seeing him, as if he'd seen a ghost? He opted to step in.

"Hey," Chad managed, before going back to his phone, which seemed to be a legitimate preoccupation.

"Hey," Brian returned, but barely, as he watched the doors close.

The elevator's four floor descent seemed to be the longest such ride Brian had ever experienced. As Chad clicked away in response to a text, Brian could only wonder if Chad had come upon this news and what he was thinking. But at least on the outside, it appeared that Chad's life remained the same as it had prior, while Brian had all but excavated his former apathetic soul and replaced it with the altruistic one that he now clutched. As the elevator slid down at a pace of molasses oozing down a brick wall, Brian could not help but remember when things had changed between them, especially now that it had just been announced that Randy Scanlon was to be released. But he resisted going back to the day itself. Instead, he summoned what he best recalled as their last *typical* exchange, just days prior to the crime.

They were side by side at the mailbox: "Friggin' Mets, huh?" Chad chuckled.

"Oh, please. Don't even get me started," Brian returned his deprecating amusement; a lifetime ago, it seemed, when Brian's life was rife with diversions such as seasonal sports. Chad too was a Mets fan, possibly to an even more obsessive degree.

"My wife'n daughter and I were there, too."

"You were at the game?"

"Oh, yeah. You could probably hear me after he dropped that fuckin' ball."

"Oh my God, I lost it, man."

"The easiest bloop, n'he was afraid to dirty his uniform."

"Right?"

"Fuckin' rich assholes. I gotta' give it up, I think," as Chad pulled out his letters.

"What, the Mets?"

"You invest all this energy in these overpriced, overrated players not fuckin' up, n'when they do, your whole week's shot."

"Hah. Good point," Brian chuckled, never really believing that Chad would ever follow through on giving up baseball – let alone the Mets. But he didn't really know him well enough to know for sure. In truth, it was the only subject they ever really discussed, aside from passing salutations in the lobby, or to complain about recently encountered transit issues. They were of the same age, and appeared to have a similar sense of humor, but they ultimately seemed to resign that they would remain as friendly neighbors in the same building without either one committing to a real friendship beyond. For Brian, it was fine. He wasn't into amassing new friends aside from the few he'd already had relationships with. He never knew where Chad stood politically. Wasn't sure what his friends were like. Wasn't sure what kind of father he was, and didn't particularly care. It was diverting banter in the lobby that took up all of 5 minutes, at most, and that was that.

To the best of his memory, that brief dialogue would be the last such exchange they would have before that fateful evening. Everything thereafter, he wanted to block out. And yet he couldn't not see them coming out of the train station at the same time, starting some banal conversation about something that Brian had now since forgotten, before they caught sight of a small assembled group on 79th Street between 35th and 36th avenue.

The elevator door opened, and Brian exited as if by gale force. It was too much to say even so much as "Take care" to Chad, especially on this day.

He arrived at Jakween's cardboarded residence, just a block and a half away, but he was nowhere to be found. He had an unpredictable schedule for a homeless person; sometimes he was there at a certain time, other times not. Perhaps he was somewhere trying to hock his Magic Bullet or some such item. Brian felt it hollow to simply leave the food inside his box, though he had done it before. But it was a feeling of gratification he was after, to see Jakween's appreciation, which could possibly make the recent news appear remote. After all, Jeff Gammon said that our past was not the whole of one's life. And Brian needed to believe that now more than ever. His story was not completely written.

He looked around, as if hoping Jakween would be en route to his depressing makeshift domicile. But there was no sign of him.

He headed back home, finally recalling that he was registered for the *Ride to Stop Domestic Abuse* tomorrow morning. He was mentally exhausted, and doubtful that he'd manage to rest enough for such an event.

In fact, that night Brian couldn't sleep. He was afraid to, as if the crime would reappear in his mind like a loathsome rerun. His phone would pull him with a fervor to search for every media post about Scanlon's impending release, as if he was seeking the article that confirmed that such news was false and that Scanlon was to serve out his complete sentence. This would lend the possibility of his own death in prison by the same brutal fashion that he inflicted on his ex-wife. In such a wish, he of course was conflicted. How the man he now was could wish death on another, even a convicted and unequivocal felon.

He soon felt queasy, and ran to the toilet to expel such feelings, which were more dry heaves since he didn't manage to eat dinner that evening and couldn't foresee when he'd have much of an appetite again.

Eight

—

Dripping sweat like rain and exhausted beyond comprehension, he pedaled past the 6-mile mark in Central Park, amidst a swarm of bikers whose energies he could only assume were well beyond his. He at least could deduce that none of them would put themselves in a position of getting virtually no sleep before a 7-mile ride in 90-degree heat. Despite this, he forced the weight of his husky legs onto the pedals, even as his mind was fatigued with any real comprehension of how much longer he had to go. But at least in eventually crossing the finish line, he felt symbolically as if he was a protector of the abused. And, of course, the donations he amassed (the entirety being from his own credit card) would be going towards that very source. In truth, any charity event Brian participated in was always a fiscal cost to himself, as he didn't feel he had close enough relationships with anyone to ask for even a modest donation. But it also would lessen his efforts for anyone but himself to make such an investment.

No one else owed him. He owed it to whatever the cause, and this one was the most important to him.

As his mind navigated lazily between his exhaustion and images of Randy Scanlon and his ex-wife, Leslie, between 35th and 36th avenue, the ambient cheers resonated like distant waves that ebbed and flowed. As he would be prone to do, he wondered how many of his fellow participants had done anything they were truly ashamed of, and were using this race against domestic abuse to help alleviate their conscience. Or if they were simply avid bikers who would seek any opportunity to partake in a marathon, regardless of the cause. But in all likelihood, they were just good people who wanted to do good, and were always like this. A kaleidoscope began to run through his head of that infamous evening, then seeing Chad in the elevator just yesterday, then Ms. Fochetti's gentle hand on his cheek, then the joy in Robert's voice at the suicide hotline, and just a soon realizing that Robert never called back the following week, which made Brian wonder if his depression had overtaken him. He struggled to navigate the good that he attempted to do over the cowardice of his past — and the very possibility that nothing he could do in the present would erase it. Throughout these abridged scenes of his past, he kept hearing Chad's neutral "Hey", which had become like an annoying fly in the lobby that would buzz in his ear on occasion only to unnerve him, as he continued pedaling — the pedals wet with his cascading perspiration, as his feet occasionally slipped.

He'd have moments of losing traction, before regaining a fourth and then fifth wind, wherein he managed to make it to a slight downward hill, allowing him to pick up momentum, as a much-needed breeze blew blissfully into his face. For the moment, he was even transported to the neighborhood bike rides of his youth in Crawberry,…before he heard –

"Hey!"

Upon hearing this, Brian simultaneously slammed on his breaks and twisted the handlebars on his 3-speed, which propelled him off the seat and smashed him onto the hot pavement…

The skids of ensuing cyclists followed…

"Are you alright?" she asked, her faceless voice strangely familiar.

"Yeah, I'm…I'm okay," he said instinctively, before even knowing who was asking.

"I'm so sorry," she followed, currently still out of his eyeshot.

"Uh…sorry for what?" he grunted…

"I feel like I threw you when I called out. I'm so sorry."

"No, you…" he managed to get his upper body elevated. "It's fine. I think I may've hit a rock or something."

"You sure?" she followed, with a heightened sense of responsibility for his descent.

"Yeah, yeah, I'm…. Ow!" he winced, as he attempted to bend his right leg, which he now noticed was gushing blood.

"Let me get you to an emergency room," her face somewhat visible to him now, though he still couldn't place her and didn't much care to, as she pulled out her phone…

"No, that's… I need to finish this…"

"What?! No way," she said without hesitation.

"Dude, you're bleeding, man," a disembodied man's voice followed…

"No, I just… It's the last mile. I can…"

"Please, don't move, okay? The more you try to move it, the more blood's gonna' come out," she gently touched his rising shoulder…

"Really, I'm…"

"You have to stay put, okay? I'll get an ambu – " she pleaded…but with a sudden rush of energy, Brian rose, retrieved his bike amidst protestations from the surrounding cyclists who had stopped…

"I'm good! I just have to finish this!" he spouted, as he awkwardly got on his bike and started to pedal… He heard the building screams of the onlookers and the stomps of footsteps urgently following him…

He woke up to the overwhelming whiteness of a hospital room, his leg now elevated and bandaged: "Hel…hello?" he feebly asked the air, uncertain if he was alive or in a strange sort of post-life limbo.

"Hey," he heard.

"He…hey," he turned his tightened neck to his right to see her. For the moment, he felt fortunate that he was not on a bike this time when she said it.

"How are you feeling?"

"I… A little achy… Where…?"

"You're at St. Luke's."

"St. Luke's?"

"You must wonder how you got here. Your bike's outside."

"How *did* I get here?"

"EMS."

"EMS brought me…? But how…? I mean, did I finish the race?"

"Finish?" she nearly laughed in astonishment. "You passed out."

"Passed out?"

"Yep," she said, with an awkward grin.

"How did that… I mean, I was on my bike…"

"Well, you *were* on your bike."

"I mean, I know I fell off, but then…"

"Yeah, you tried to get back on but passed out right after, I'm afraid."

His disappointment sinking in. "My God,… I didn't even finish."

"Well, yeah, but…you're alive. That's more of an upshot, isn't it?" she smiled.

He pondered this, "Yeah, I guess."

"It coulda' been worse."

He took this in, still processing his lack of memory. "Where's my stuff?"

"Oh, everything's here, on the chair. I had to use your wallet to give them your identification and insurance info, but it's all there."

He strained to look over in the vicinity of where his stuff was, before coming back to her.

"I appreciate you're helping me, but… I'm sorry, what's your name?"

"Vanessa," she said, with a smile that was mainly what Brian recognized.

"Yeah, that's… I didn't know your name, but we've met before, right?"

"*Legs Against Lupus*, right. I saw you and called out'n… Shit, I'm really sorry."

"Don't…hey, don't worry about it."

"If I knew your name then, I would've just said your name instead of *'Hey'*. Maybe that would've been less distracting," she said, half jesting.

"Uh,…it doesn't really matter. I just really want to leave here."

"Well, the doctor said he'd check in again. You were out, so…"

"Okay, but I… I really need to go."

"You should really wait for a doctor."

He momentarily ceased his urge to get out of bed, processing the events that happened, while finding it strange that Vanessa, as he now knew her, felt confident enough despite how little they knew each other to call out to him as if they were neighbors. They had only met the one time, and it was hardly what one would call a meeting. It was small talk that Brian barely partook in.

He was further unsettled by her commitment to want to take some sort of responsibility for his care, even more so as she looked at him, mystified: "Why did you want to finish so bad?"

He looked at her, oddly. "What?"

"I mean, you were bleeding, and you kept saying you had to finish, like you were in a scene from *Breaking Away*."

He was reluctant to answer. "I just… I like to finish what I start, that's all. And I'm done being cared for here, so I'd like to finish that, too. I'm sorry, do you mind grabbing a nurse?"

"Sure. I get ya'. I hate these places, too. But listen to what they tell you, okay? From experience. I just wouldn't be so quick to leave until you know what's what."

"Don't *you* know what's what?"

"Whata' you mean?"

"They didn't do anything yet?"

"No, they just said you had a bad gash. You'd probably need stitches, but I couldn't authorize anything. They'll talk to ya'. I'll be back with a nurse, okay?"

"Thank you," he managed, then allowed his back to momentarily sink into the bed, though he was still uneasy with his circumstances and felt vulnerable in how these recent events unfolded. What was worse for him was a feeling of abject failure; of not fulfilling his goal of completing the 7-mile race, combined with his current immobility, was something he couldn't explain to anyone. For the first time in a while, he was in utter despair.

Approximately two feet from the bed was his backpack. Its proximity amplified an urgency to have it closer to him, but not because he was concerned that Vanessa or someone else may have taken something, but because his phone was there – and through his phone he could access Jeff Gammon's voice. And within it, he hoped to have some value as to his place on the earth restored. He attempted to reach his hand out to his bag, but he was nowhere near close enough to retrieve it. He then slid his aching body slowly so that his right hip was flush against the bed rail, but he was still not close enough. The thought of waiting for someone to return became out of the question, as his desperation grew. *How pathetic*, he thought. *I couldn't even finish. Those poor women. All they've been through, and I couldn't even finish for them.*

Before he would make his next attempt, he stopped, took a breath as if to slow the barrage of negative thoughts, then recalled one of his mantras, which he whispered to himself: "My story is not yet written. My story is not yet written. My story is not yet written..."

He stopped just as Vanessa came in, followed by the nurse.

Nine

—

He felt weird about departing so quickly after being released, so he indulged Vanessa by allowing her to treat him to lunch at a diner near the hospital. He appreciated her kindness, but nevertheless there was an awkwardness as to where it stemmed from: if she felt guilty because she inadvertently derailed him off his bike which resulted in six stitches on his shin, or something else.

"At least they'll be off in a coupla' weeks," as he picked at his tuna melt, his stitched right leg extended along his booth seat.

"Yeah, you'll be okay. Again, Brian, I'm…"

"Please, Vanessa, you don't have to apologize anymore. I told you that it was probably a rock or something anyway," he fibbed, unable to look at her.

"I don't believe you," she grinned.

He then looked at her with a tepid smile, "Vanessa, please."

"Alright, alright. I'll stop."

"Thanks," he weakly appreciated.

"But thanks for letting me get lunch, at least."

"You really didn't have to."

"I wanted to. My God, you show up intending to just donate your time to an important cause, and you end up with your leg in a sling. After all that, the least you deserve is a free tuna melt. Jeez…" as she dug into her giant Greek salad.

"I just wish…" he mused, but caught himself before he continued.

"What?"

"Nothing, it's all good."

"Why do I feel like you're beating up yourself about this?"

He paused. "About what?"

"Not finishing."

He looked at her, surprised at the observation, then looked down at his plate. "I'm…I'm not."

"Your intentions were there. Not everyone finishes these things."

"I guess I just put a lot of things in my way, and I'm not pleased with myself that I did."

"Like what?"

Every time Vanessa asked a question, or a follow up, it gave Brian pause for the very reason that it challenged him to either tell the truth or fabricate in a way that would somehow lessen her intrigue – but he wasn't a savvy enough conversationalist to navigate this particularly well. "I mean, I was on no sleep, I was exhausted, and, still, I almost… Anyway," he stopped himself again, but could no longer eat when recalling all the things that had been distressing him.

Vanessa observed this, taking a bite from her salad before speaking again: "Were you one of those guys who was a real jock as a kid? Trophies'n all that?" she smiled.

Reluctantly, he replied: "No, I was... I mean, I played sports, yeah. Yeah, I guess I was a bit of a... But this has nothing to do with that. I don't even follow sports anymore."

"Well, people have a competitive nature. It doesn't just leave you."

"Well, it did," he said, not harshly but somewhat defensively. His failure at the cycling event had little to do with his old desires to win a game he was playing. When he played sports as a kid or even pick-up basketball with Lucas and his old friends, he wanted to win. Wanted to not only assist but to be the primary scorer, as if his stats would somehow end up in the *New York Post*. But those days were, in fact, gone. Those tendencies belonged to someone else. In who he was now was only a desire to accomplish something that would benefit someone else. That was his victory.

As energetic and youthful as Vanessa seemed, there was an intuitiveness to her that seemed beyond her years, which intimidated Brian. He sensed that nothing with her could be on the surface, unless she lost interest in probing. At least that was what he was getting. She then followed, "Okay. Then…do you mind if I ask why you're so hard on yourself?"

Brian could not help but be taken aback, yet again, since he really didn't have people in his life who would question his behavior. Since Sara, really. And here was another woman, and one he didn't know well. And certainly one who did not know his past self; the self who would always prefer a brainless diversion over anything even remotely resembling charity. He couldn't possibly let her know how guilt-ridden he was, which kept him up the previous night, and the kaleidoscopic images that were circulating in front of him before she called out to him. This was one of many reasons why it was easier for him to go through life giving of himself, being kind to people without committing to a relationship beyond the altruistic. He didn't need to know someone well any more than he wanted anyone to know him.

He looked at her, her sincere brown eyes committed to know his answer, as her fork dangled over her plate, before he reached for his coffee with feigned nonchalance… "It's just…how I am. Go figure, y'know?" He sipped, allowing the cup to remain before his lips, as Vanessa took this in, unsure of what to believe.

"I'm sorry, I feel like I'm asking these deep questions, but I'm not intending for them to be particularly deep," she weakly chuckled.

"It's fine. Hey, we're just talking, right?"

"Right. But, really, if I'm being too…"

"No, it's fine," then with an attempt to change course, "Hey, this is very nice of you, to take me out to lunch. I just want you to know…"

"Oh, please."

"No, really. Thank you," he smiled at her, but couldn't quite sustain it to the extent that she could not read some sort of torment in him.

"Well,…you're very welcome, Brian," she said, with an attempted seriousness intended to match his sincere appreciation. She went back to her salad, as he went back to his sandwich. Then… "Did you have to be somewhere?"

"Why do you ask?"

"You jus' seemed a little anxious at the hospital."

"No, I was… I guess I was just anxious to get outa' there, y'know?" he weakly chuckled.

"Sure, I hear ya'."

They resumed eating, then somehow Brian felt compelled to expound… "I was hoping to make it to church, but…" he trailed off, as he took another bite.

"You go to church?"

"Yeah. When I can't make the Sunday masses, I at least like to go to confession."

"Confession?" Vanessa couldn't help but cease the motion of her fork to her mouth at this.

"Yeah. Why?"

"No, just… I guess I just don't encounter a lot of diehard churchgoers. Wasn't sure they really existed anymore under 75. But now it makes sense." she smiled, as she ate.

"What makes sense?"

"Catholic guilt, right? You can't just be disappointed. You have to put a boulder on your back," she snickered.

"No, that's not… It's not about being Catholic."

"No?" she asked, now regretting her assumption.

"I mean, yeah, I was raised Catholic, but I don't have any religious…   I just…feel good when I go," he replied, bashfully, as he twirled his coleslaw with his fork.

"Hm," she took this in. "Well, good for you. That's kinda' refreshing, actually."

"Thanks," he responded timidly.

"You chant too?"

"Chant?"

"I heard you when I came in with the nurse. I thought I heard you repeating something."

Brian blushed at this. He didn't think she heard him reciting his variation on one of Jeff Gammon's mantras, *My story is not yet written.* He barely knew how to respond.

She saw the redness in his face come as if an allergic reaction. "I'm sorry. Should I've not…?"

"No, no, it's… I just didn't think you heard," as he stirred his already well-stirred coffee.

"If it's personal, we can – "

"It's a mantra. I just repeat it when I'm… I don't usually say it aloud, but I was just stressing a little."

"Why?"

"The hospital, everything. I was unconscious, I arrived there out of the blue. It was…"

"Yeah, I hear ya'. It was disorienting."

"Yeah,…it was."

"Hey, whatever works, I say. A mantra beats a meltdown," she smiled, then ate a drenched piece of lettuce.

Brian was struck by her phrasing. "That's good."

"Yeah, it is, isn't it. I think that'll be my next T-shirt."

"Your next T-shirt?"

"Yeah. I design them. I don't make a living at it. It's mainly for myself and people who find them interesting."

She then removed her *Ride to Stop Domestic Abuse* shirt under which was one of her own, with *Life is Like Flying in Economy Class – There's No Room for Baggage* emblazoned across her chest, which Brian read sheepishly, as if he were peeping.

"Hm, that's… Yeah, well… Pretty true, I'd say."

"Thanks. I think so too."

Brian then recalled the shirt she wore when they initially met at the *Legs Against Lupus* walkathon, which he remembered as seeming like a spin on Forrest Gump: *Life is Like a Box – It's All About What*

You Put Inside, and now assumed she had designed that one as well.

As she went back to her salad, she managed to continue the thread of their conversation prior. "I don't consider myself religious, really. But I did study Theology, for a bit. Now I try'n practice Buddhism, so that's as close as I get. I'm erratic, but I try. I mean, I chant. I meet with a group once a month. I have a gohonzon. But my beliefs are sort of a pastiche, y'know? Different things, different sources, but I find that the more you read these things, the more they all seem to come back to the same thing."

"And what's that?" he asked, now more interested in knowing her answer than deflecting her questions.

"Well,...we all want peace in our lives, right? Lack of conflict. More love. Less judgement. We want to have an idea of what's after this," she crunched a crouton loudly, as if the exclamation.

"Any ideas?" he weakly smiled.

"Oh, God, I dunno'," she chuckled. "I think we all will what we want it to be, right?"

Brian thought on this, not knowing himself. "I guess."

"Don't you?"

He looked at her. "I dunno'. I guess I've tried not to give it much thought. I'm still figuring out what all *this* is."

She laughed, then "That's the joke, isn't it."

"What do you mean?"

"Just…whether we'll have long enough to figure it out or if we'll die still not understanding what the hell it was all about," she smiled, but not flippantly. Brian couldn't help but be intrigued at how she could phrase things that, for him, still seemed overwhelming; such as how his life would end and what knowledge he would amass at that point. Not to mention the after-life, if one existed.

Then, as if the subject of death was a bit much for him, he reluctantly brought things back to life in the present: "Our story is not yet written," he dared to utter, before sipping his coffee.

"What's that?"

"Just…a paraphrase. Something I like to quote. Jeff Gammon. *My story is not yet written.* I find it helpful."

Her eyes narrowed at this, "Hm, I know him."

"You've read him?" as his confidence seemed to increase with their conversation…

"A little, but I stopped."

Brian asked with a mouthful, "Why?"

"You haven't heard about him?"

He swallowed, "Heard what?"

"Well, it's allegations. They never proved any-thing. But there were articles about him that sorta' soured me."

"What articles?"

"They came out back in, like, 2018. Some women who'd worked for him that he allegedly groped'n whatnot. You never heard about this?"

Brian's heart nearly stopped, "No."

"Well, I haven't seen anything since. But I just thought it was unsettling to hear."

"It doesn't mean that it's true," Brian said, adamantly.

Vanessa could not help but pick up on his sudden conviction. "No, you're right. It wasn't just that. To be honest, before I even heard that, I was already feeling that he came off a little…."

"A little what?" he asked, somewhat defensively.

"A little…self-righteous. But that's just me. You know some of these self-help folks can sometimes get in front of their messages, and I started to feel he was doing that."

"Well, I think you're wrong. I saw him speak last year. He was amazing."

"Okay, well, I'm glad – "

"I mean, everyone has their own path, and…and we should respect those paths, don't you think?" as he needlessly stirred his coffee again.

"I agree – "

"And if it hasn't been proven that he abused women, then…"

"Brian, I'm not saying you're endorsing that."

"My God, are you kidding?!" he said louder, which prompted Vanessa to look around sheepishly at the surrounding patrons. "I'm sorry," he lowered his voice. "It's... He brought me out of a... I was going through...kind of a tough period when I read one of his books, and it just...helped."

"I understand," she said softly, and it appeared she did.

He then managed, with forced jubilance: "This is nice. Good tuna melt. Thanks." Brian couldn't lift his head to assure her more than his words, as he took another hollow bite.

She looked at him, before turning back to her plate, picking at her lettuce. "Hey, it's nice to explore things, y'know? I give you credit. It's always better to believe in something than nothing. And, trust me, I went some years believing just that."

"Nothing?"

"Sure."

He reluctantly agreed, "Me too," before sipping more coffee...

"Yeah?" she brightly asked.

Brian again regretted leaving himself open for more probing. While it was not unlike when Robert asked him about what prompted him to start reading the *I Ching*, Brian could mask himself at the suicide hotline. He could fabricate and his invisibility could conceal what was false well enough. But before Vanessa's eyes, it was more challenging, even to be vague. He took a moment. "Well, yeah. I mean, I had a stretch where, frankly, I didn't really give it much thought."

"What?"

"Just…religion. Spirituality. It just wasn't something I thought about or wanted to give my time to."

"So…what changed?"

He paused again, trying to remain composed to her curiosity, which again led her to stop eating and give her complete focus to his answer. "Well, just…life, y'know?" He felt a certain success in his vagueness.

She took this in, "Sure," then swallowed a cherry tomato.

"What about you?" he followed, obviously deflecting, but not without interest.

She took a moment herself, which seemed like the first time she needed to muse on her response, as if wanting to phrase something carefully. "Well, okay, this might be a lot for a first lunch, but…I almost died," she said, though more like a punchline than a morbid revelation.

"Really?" Brian again stopped eating.

"Yep," as she resumed eating, no doubt as an intent of diluting the seriousness.

"How? I'm sorry, do you mind if I…?"

"It's fine. So I was born with some issues, which sort of developed as I got a little older. Then when everyone thought I was out of the woods, they returned. I had BPD."

"What's…?"

"Remember this for the next Scrabble game, okay?: Bronchiopulmonary dysplasia."

As he tried to absorb all the letters, "Jesus, I've never heard of it."

"Yeah, it doesn't exactly have the cache' of some other diseases but…it exists," she popped an olive into her mouth, then… "They said it might've been genetic from my birth mother. I was adopted. So anyway, a lot of my early years were in hospitals, so that's why I'm sort of familiar with them," she then inhaled a crouton. "Then I went through some angry adult years of questioning things.   You know, why was I put up for adoption? Why was I born sick? Why was I this'n that? Started drinking a little too much. All completely and utterly untherapeutic. Anyway, it wasn't until the last three years or so that I started to realize what almost happened to me."

"What happened?"

"Well, I saw a psychologist for a bit, which was helpful until it wasn't. But when it was, I found I was able to reconnect with myself as a child. Memories. And I remembered that I almost died."

"Really?"

"And more accurately, *did* die."

"What?"

"Yep."

"How…do you know that?"

"Well, I remember that I saw a light."

"A light? Like…?"

"Yeah, it's the light you hear a lot of people mention who've had near-death experiences. I mean, it was brief, so I can't say I have any real post-life experience, or that I jammed with John Lennon or anything. But there was something in recalling that that made me live my life differently after that. The biggest thing was, well, that I didn't feel connected to most people in my life. You know?"

"Uh,…yeah, I… Sure."

"I mean, I had friends, I had a boyfriend, but all our communication, the bulk of it, was through our phones, through other sources, but we weren't really having conversations anymore. Like this. And what was sad was that I found a lot of the people in my life didn't have time to do like we're doing here. Or if we did, they were still on their phones or just generally distracted. My mother, my *adoptive* mother, always said I was an old soul, so that gives you some context as to why I sound like I'm 80," she snickered. "I just realized, life is short. I know that, probably more than most, because…I guess my life was almost, like, *really* short. So…what can I do? So I still had asthma. I still had respiratory issues. I'm still someone who was given away by a mother who I no longer care to find. I still have some other things but, shit, I'm alive. So I started to donate my time to causes that meant something to me, started reading more. Went back to school. Read theological stuff, spiritual stuff, existential stuff. Got into Buddhism. Started to give back, 'cause there's always someone who has it worse than you, right?" she smiled at this, realizing she must have sounded like a bumper sticker. "But it's true, right?"

"I…yeah," Brian managed, still consumed by her revelations.

She chewed on a piece of lettuce, then swallowed. "There's no obligation here, okay?"

"I… What do you mean?"

"With this. I just wanted to take you to lunch. We might not speak again after this, and that's fine. That's how human relations go. I get it. It's just connecting. You were there, at the Lupus walk. Seemed nice. That's all." She bit into another crouton. "And then I almost killed you," she grinned.

Brian didn't even catch her jest at the end because he found himself transfixed by her words leading up to it, realizing it had been a long time before he sat across from someone and listened to them. And, quite possibly, never had he sat across from someone who revealed why they were how they were without a sense of bitterness towards the world. There was something nourishing about her openness, even if he still couldn't help but wonder why him. But he had less of a reason to speculate now because it seemed that this was just how she was. He was nothing special. She was just a nice person. And he was there. And when he thought that, he suddenly felt less awkward than unworthy of her presence. Because not only was she triumphing over the adversity of her health issues and being orphaned, he also realized that her urge to give back was not unlike his – except the inspiration for it was vastly different. He struggled to respond to all she had revealed to him, wanting to even ask her if she'd ever been ashamed, before thinking better of it. Eventually, he managed: "So how…how are you feeling now?" he almost whispered.

"You mean healthwise?" she asked.

"Yeah."

"Pretty good, actually. Most days. Everything's pretty controllable. I have my pump, so I try to be smart with my limitations."

Observing her heretofore unimpeded energy and positivity. "Well, you really don't seem to be affected by it."

"Well, I can have a salad," she smiled.

"No, I mean, come on. You're doing walkathons and 7-mile cycling events…"

"Well, I didn't finish that one."

"You could've."

She took a beat, "And so could *you* have," her eyes focused on his, as if to assure him, which he (and perhaps she) did not see coming.

Vanessa wasn't going to blame herself again for Brian's fall, but more to her point, at least it seemed, was that finishing such an event did not detract from the effort. She didn't know why Brian felt the way he did and why it meant so much to him, but it seemed that she somehow wanted to convey that there were different victories. While it might not have curbed his guilt or erased what she had noted about his remote mentor Jeff Gammon, it certainly made him admire her, regardless of what their relationship was to become.

Ten

—

With his leg still tender, he nevertheless went back to work on Monday. It was unfathomable to him to take time off, especially since the diversion of work was appreciated now more than ever. He could do without the odd climate within the office, but resigned that it was just as easy to get work done without much interaction. Even easier, actually. In truth, it was really only in specialty situations where such communication was warranted, and it usually would come from Ismet, particularly if a name needed to be removed from the database – usually stemming from a recipient moving to some sort of assisted living or nursing home facility, or, more commonly, their death. Brian, Tim and Shanda all had authorization to make such adjustments, as long as the office received some sort of correspondence from either the family or building management.

And so things proceeded as usual: Tim swigged Mountain Dew and mumbled on a call with a typically anonymous friend as he numbly entered in data.

Shanda had her unwaveringly throbbing music in her ears. While Brian listened to Jeff Gammon; often replaying the same passages over again, as if it were his oxygen. Most notably: *"Everyone has their own story. And our stories aren't just our past. They're the entirety of our lives. Not just what we fall into but what we become through our own efforts. But the only thing that really matters is what your story is."*

That evening he worked a shift at the suicide hotline. As was often the case, he'd read or listen to Jeff Gammon while waiting for a first call to come in, which sometimes could take as long as an hour or so into his shift. Despite the distractions in his life, he made sure that all that he was reading or listening to was placing him in the best possible mindset to deal with someone who was in crisis. And yet, he still could not get out of his head how it'd been three weeks since his conversation with Robert, to whom he read a passage from the *I Ching*, which had appeared to inspire him to the extent that he was looking forward to speaking with Brian further about it. But he'd heard nothing. Brian would ask the other volunteers in the room if they'd heard from him and none had spoken to a "Robert" within that time. So he could only speculate as to what had happened. Did Robert simply no longer feel compelled to speak about his depression? Was he over it? Did the book really help him? *Or did he actually…?*

He was also fighting the compulsion to check on the status of Randy Scanlon's release. The internet had revealed nothing new, per his searches. And he wondered what it mattered, to know exactly when he was getting out, other than the fact that he wanted to know when the man would be free. *And what then?* How would that change him, to know that this man could resume his life after serving a mere 18 months for his ex-wife's death? These thoughts continued to creep in between Jeff Gammon's reassuring sentences.

He didn't give much thought to Vanessa since the post-bike-accident lunch yesterday. It wasn't that he didn't find her memorable or appreciate her company, but it seemed that much more daunting for him to incorporate her into all the other stuff that was pulling at him. To add someone, particularly a woman, who nearly died at birth, who was still dealing with respiratory issues and God knows what else, who still could've finished a 7-mile charity race if it weren't for his stupidity, was all but overwhelming. They exchanged numbers, but he didn't see himself calling her.

Then he thought of when he'd see Chad again,…and if he'd heard by now that Scanlon was to be released… And then his line beeped. He turned off the audiobook in his ears, placed on his hotline headset, took a breath, then picked up – he'd hoped it was Robert.

"Hi, I need to talk to someone," he said. His voice sounding similar; male, late teens or early twenties.

"Well, I'm happy to hear you. My name's Brian," he said, summoning all his energy to be comforting, and even glad that he could shift his energies to be there for someone.

"Thank you, Brian."

"Sure, sure. Would you like to tell me your name?" he asked.

"Uh, sure. It's…it's Steven."

"Hi, Steven. How're you?"

"Well, you know,…a little sweaty."

Brian didn't expect such a description, but assumed this could be a person who might not be able to afford their electric bill. "Well, yeah, I get that."

"Do you?"

"Uh, sure. It's July. It's gettin' up there, right?" he said with a smile.

"Up where?" the caller asked, as if suppressing a giggle.

Brian paused. "Well, you know, temperature-wise. It's hot."

"Oh, I see. I thought you meant 'up there' as in UP YOUR ASS, FUCKWAD!" before a cacophony of adolescent snickers followed, which then clicked off.

No, it certainly wasn't Robert. It wasn't anyone he could help. It was a prank phone call, which occurred from time to time – even at a suicide hotline. Brian sat there, not angered but only dejected – especially when recalling that that was the kind of thing *he* might've done as a teenager.

*****

The week continued not unlike previous weeks. He was more in the field than the office but, thankfully, when he was there it was all fairly seamless. By contrast, it was as if the habits of his fellow staff and the daily occurrences were like a well-oiled wheel that was unlikely to be derailed anytime soon.

On one of his field assessments, he arrived at the apartment of Delia Warden, a former actress of limited success who now lived by herself in an apartment that was left to her by her parents some years ago. Her story was that she had run out of money and could no longer afford to maintain her apartment on the upper east side of Manhattan, not long after her banker husband was arrested. He'd left her nothing, since his assets were seized due to a Ponzi scheme that he was the chief architect of. Many people lost their life savings. She barely had time to absorb her own sense of guilt about living off her husband's crimes before he would die of a heart attack in prison. She had no children. And now she was housebound by crippling arthritis in the modest apartment that she was raised in:

"They say you can't go home again. You ever heard that?" she snapped from her recliner, clutching a brandy and a cigarette.

"Uh, yes. I have," he awkwardly agreed.

"Well, it's obviously a damned lie. 'Cause here I am. I came back thinking I'd at least have my health, and now I can't move outa' here. Not only am I home again, I'm part a' the damn furniture."

Many of these people could be categorized as cantankerous, especially if they still had their wits about them. Ms. Warden indeed did, which made her dormancy that much more frustrating for her. Brian could sense her blend of resentment and remorse, which occasionally seeped out of their exchange.

"I was never a great actress, Brian. But I was good, y'know?"

"I'm sure you were, Ms. Warden," he tepidly assured.

"I didn't do Broadway or a lot of films or TV, but I did some things that I was proud of. I worked until I didn't. And I *didn't* when I got older and was sick of playing grandmothers before I was even 50. My husband became who I was, unfortunately. He made the money. He took us on trips. We went everywhere. And somehow that made my own lack of success less painful. Then I heard about what he'd done, and…and all I had was a sick feeling. No career. No kids. Just rage and regret. And now I barely have legs," she took a sip. "It's all a penance. I don't even believe in God, and yet I believe in penance. Isn't that something? The things we do, whether we're responsible or not… I think it comes back to us. My idiot husband was my identity, and so his karma's mine," she sat with this, seeming to have said this to the air many times, and perhaps to visiting nurses who ignored her.

Brian was still in the mode of being a professional case worker. He'd heard unsettling things from people, witnessed their depression and physical limitations, and could still manage to be focused in these situations. Even respectfully consoling, if need be. "You shouldn't feel responsible, Ms. Warden. You didn't know. This doesn't have anything to do with what your husband did, I'm sure," he tried to assert, though he could not know, and always felt odd in making such declarations, even if it was from a place of trying to lessen one's despair.

At this point, Ms. Warden had answered all the pertinent questions. Brian's words of consolation appeared to have little effect, as she gazed out the window onto the busy afternoon street. As she did, he could not help but notice several old oil paintings leaned up against the walls that were replaced by framed show posters, as if to assert that she once had a career. He was particularly struck by one of the play titles, *You Can't Take It With You*, which in the moment appeared to have particular relevance.

He placed the paperwork in his shoulder bag, and rose with the one bit of assurance that he could offer, that her application would indeed be approved and that deliveries for her would start the following week, to which she puckered a quick smile that vanished just as quickly.

As he started towards the door, she called out suddenly: "Brian?"

He stopped, stepped towards her: "Yes, mam," as he smiled eagerly.

She then turned to him. "Have you ever done anything that you're ashamed of?"

A chill went up his spine. While it likely was intended as a question she was asking to absolve her own sense of compunction, it appeared to Brian as if Delia Warden's spirit had been somehow replaced by something else.

Eleven

—

Still in somewhat of a daze from his visit to Delia Warden's earlier in the day, he dropped off food to Jakween, who was God-knows-where in the neighborhood. Nevertheless, it was a small comfort to Brian to see him active and, perhaps, even *pro*active towards a better life, which he wanted to take a small amount of credit for. But the day still added to his increased imbalance. He had hoped to see Father Devon for confession, but it was impossible during the week given his work schedule and the limited church hours, and so he bottled the feelings that were still very much within him, and were becoming exacerbated. He wasn't nearly prepared to reveal the sources of his guilt to anyone, not even a priest in a darkened booth who didn't even know his name, but still had a desperate need to tell someone just enough in the hopes of hearing back a reassurance that he was a sinner not unlike any sinner of the earth. And that in being such, one could not be expected to live with a boulder on one's back, as Vanessa had joked, let alone push one up a mountain like Sisyphus.

Maybe he could've said something to Delia Warden that would've both proven a salve to her while helping himself, but he was rendered speechless. It was so unexpected that he was still reeling from her question. The more he thought about it, the more he realized that there really was no one else he could speak to about what was plaguing him; except, perhaps,…to Chad.

He sat on his aged couch in the middle of his increasingly lonely apartment, its silence a necessity, and pondered if initiating a conversation with Chad would be helpful, in some way. After all, Chad was the only one who Brian actually knew who saw what Chad saw. Chad was also the only one who knew Brian was there; the other seemingly faceless onlookers were more representative of the diverse if ineffectual community in which they lived. He began to dwell on what the benefits of this interaction would be, since he would mainly feel compelled on the basis of his own guilt. But if Chad felt the same, or close to it at least to the extent that their opening up about the harrowing event could bear some mutual fruit, then it certainly wouldn't be for naught. If he could at least have a vague confessional exchange with Father Devon prior, he might feel more confident in this idea. He didn't feel he could do it, otherwise.

His cell phone alerted that a message had come into his voicemail – it was Vanessa, whose name and number he had programmed into his phone. Somehow he thought he'd hear from her again, but was more loath to the thought than welcoming of it. He didn't even want to play the message, and, instead, chose to listen to Jeff Gammon's *The Benevolent You* chapter entitled "Overcoming the Invisible", as he closed his eyes and leaned into the couch pillows:

"I once thought that success was equated by what I attracted. Money. Property. Cars. Travelling. And that is sort of an American Dream, isn't it. We've heard it forever. The billboard of success: to live without encumbrances. To live without any constraints. Because we think it's so tragic when we don't have enough money to buy things that we want. We think it's so sad when we have to scrimp and save. Those limitations, we feel, are our failures. But they're not. What they are, more than anything, are faux obstacles. Faux meaning not real. Invisible. So you ask, 'Well, but I'd like to be more comfortable and less stressed, and that comes from having more money.' Well, the reality is that most of us may not truly ever have enough to be comfortable, let alone be rich. So once we establish that, are we supposed to say 'Well, that's that, then. I mean, what's the point?' But that is the point. The point is that life is momentary, but it is still your story to tell. And wouldn't it

be incredibly boring if all our stories were the same? I was bored, and I was monetarily rich. Now I feel more alive than ever because I actually rid myself of that, and now I'm emotionally rich. And so maybe you never had monetary wealth, it doesn't mean that you can't have emotional wealth. Spiritual wealth. Maybe you feel that what you haven't done in your life up to this point dictates what you can do for the rest of it. Or the mistakes of your past are preventing you from what good you can still do. These are faux obstacles. They are not there. Now you don't have to drop everything and volunteer in Sudan for the rest of your life. But you can make changes within your life that give it greater value. And that value is given based on what you can give to someone else. For as long as you're alive,...it is all within you."

Brian sat with this. More than the impact of the words that he heard was now the question of what he would do if he didn't have Jeff Gammon, as his life now seemed as if it were reconstructed by sages who he'd come to so rely upon. It unsettled him more to conceive of his life without their stabilizing philosophies. He was living a better life. Everything he was hearing from Gammon made sense, in the end. Everything he was watching, reading. It all made sense. He was better for it all, without question.

And yet, he was clinging.

Twelve

His minimal sleep would force him up earlier than usual on Saturday morning. At his dining table, he wrote on a piece of paper:

Hey, Chad – It's Brian from 4C. I hope you and your family are well. How about those Mets?

He balked at this, for he no longer knew how the Mets were, having stopped watching their games. And he felt deceitful in easing back into some sort of communication with Chad on the basis of what connected them in the past. He crossed out the last sentence, then:

I know it's been a while since we've chatted in the lobby, and I'll admit that it's been my fault. I've been going through some things

He looked at this, and could think of nothing else to add. It was challenging to write a letter to someone whom he did not know well, and had pretty much been avoiding. He felt that Chad must have known why, but, again, this was never a friend of his. This was a neighbor with whom he periodically engaged in mindless small talk, which made attempts at initiating any sort of exchange that much more difficult. And if Chad refused, wouldn't that make things all the more unbearable for Brian in that building?

He slid the paper across the table in embarrassment over his wording, then grabbed his coffee mug and went to the window overlooking the children's playground. By then, the assemblage of young children accompanied by one or both parents had started. It was one of the meditative practices that eased him into his day at the office on Saturdays. The oceanic sounds of children oblivious to the ills of the world always managed to sedate him, as he continued to look at the playground like revisiting slight variations of the same painting. But on this day, there was something unique. Within a few minutes, the man with the fedora and shoulder bag entered. In the last few weeks, he had noticed him sitting on a bench in the playground with a book, always assuming he was related to one of the kids, without ever seeing him interact with any of them. But now Brian watched him enter the park and saw that the man was alone, unaccompanied by any children. Questions ran through him regarding if the man was there during the week, when Brian wasn't observing. He assumed the man probably worked and possibly didn't have the time to do so, except for Saturday. But now that it looked as if the man was frequenting the playground without children of his own, the real question was why he was there. Was this simply a clueless individual unphased by his surroundings and the exclamatory sign that clearly prohibited adults unaccompanied by children in the park? Or was this someone with an unfathomable motive?

Brian watched the man sit at the usual bench, pull out his paperback, and he wondered what he should do. His legs locked, suddenly; an immobility he instantly recalled from observing the attack on Leslie Scanlon. His mind was awash in how to proceed, but nothing seemed to make sense. At the moment, he didn't feel there was anything rational he could do except go to work.

Arriving at Ms. Fochetti's apartment for her delivery that afternoon, things proceeded as they often would; the tingling in his nostrils upon his entrance into her darkened lair, her hoarding unaltered. She'd ask him to place the meals on her counter, still disguised by her knick-knacks, old newspapers and catalogs. And, in what had become equally habitual, he would accidentally place the food on the tail of the camouflaged Socrates, whose brown, tan and white pattern would promptly scamper off the counter with his three legs like a feline tripod, before fading into the darkness – concluding with Brian's series of eruptive sneezes.

This particular ritual had now become welcoming in its predictability, almost to the point where Brian felt he was no longer experiencing his visits in the present. He did try to bring up something different or come upon a new discovery in his visits, such as noticing Socrates' absent limb, which would serve as a stimulus for Ms. Fochetti, and indeed it appeared to work, as it led her to tell the story of how she rescued him. But on this day, there was nothing unusual other than what had already been established, and he knew his lack of inspiration could be attributed to a certain distraction he was fighting; Randy Scanlon, Chad, the mysterious man in the children's playground, his still tender leg. He didn't want to mention her kids or her TV diversions or offering to help clean her apartment again, but he was at a loss of what else he could say and somehow did not want to leave her without some distinction to this visit.

As his visit was approaching its logical conclusion, she would touch Brian's cheek, as per usual; "Such a good young man you are", before he suddenly felt the urge to touch hers for the first time, then looked deeply into her gray eyes as never before, and said "Ms. Fochetti,…I just want you to know that I care about you," and then he hugged her.

A surge of deep emotion began to replace the same urge to sneeze, but he controlled it all, even as she wrapped her boney, frail arms around him with unexpected force, as if she knew something.

Thirteen

—

He sat in the front pew on Sunday, as Father Devon concluded: "God has given each one of us at this mass today the ultimate gift of life. He has said to us '*This is yours to do what you will*'. And we go from there. Now some of us may go through life being attentive to those words, and some of us may not hear them. Remember that Jesus told the story of the shepherd who lost one of his hundred sheep, and how the shepherd could not live knowing one was lost. When he found that lost sheep, it proved the point that Jesus was making, which is that everything lost can be found. And that there is no less value to the life of one who may've went astray. God is with you."

Brian sat with this, clutching his hands together, ignoring the surrounding nodding parishioners and caterwauling infants. Again, he wanted to believe that Father Devon was speaking directly to him, since it was the best way for him not to feel lost. That his efforts of an improved and altruistic life was visible to God, even if he didn't consider himself a particular denomination but more of a collective goodness tethered to religion and spiritual philosophy, since that was how he seized his self-education.

Shortly after mass, Brian went to the confessional booth but was quickly dismayed by a sign outside which noted that the confessional would be closed. He couldn't conceive of what would deter something so sacred to him, especially now. He even waited outside the church before seeing Father Devon escorted into his car. Such urgency from a man he had heretofore only observed walking and speaking at such a leisurely pace within the church walls was stunning to him. He asked an usher within the church if he knew why the confessional was closed, to which the response was whispered, "Last rites."

Brian knew that this meant someone was near-death, and Father Devon was likely going to be one of the last faces they would see, as he would give blessings that, he assumed, would admit them to their soul's next existence. Since he was at church, he felt it odd to believe that it would be anywhere but Heaven,…but just as quickly began to wonder if it would be somewhere else, beyond what the Father would ever reveal.

What was further concerning was that Brian felt a need to speak with Chad, but wanted some sort of endorsement from the Father, even if he never planned to go into specifics. But now it seemed foolish that Brian should wait to speak with him in confession. Perhaps everything that day occurred as it did to ultimately put everything in Brian's hands; to empower him to find the words to write to Chad, and simply allow Brian to be at ease with whatever the outcome would be. Perhaps it would end with the letter he'd place under Chad's door. Or maybe he wouldn't hear anything and that would be that. Then it would just come down to Brian's instinctive feeling on if it was worth staying in that building, while continuing to evade that fateful block.

He had little choice, it seemed, but to do what compelled him.

That evening, he placed a short one page note under Chad's door on the 5th floor. He knew his apartment by his lobby mailbox, though it felt strange to be up there. Nevertheless, the seed was planted. The final draft of his note read:

Hey, Chad - It's Brian, from 4C. I hope you and your family are well. I know this may be a little strange, but I wondered if you'd like to meet for coffee sometime soon, if there's a time that works for you. I have something I'd like to ask you and feel doing so in person would be the best way to do it. Please let me know if there's a good time. You can text or call me.

Brian provided his number, and that was that. There were several drafts of his note, which he ultimately whittled down to something that was more enigmatic, which he felt was the best approach. If he said too much, he was putting himself in a more vulnerable position, particularly if Chad chose to not respond. This way, he felt Chad would be walking into their meeting with his resistance lowered, at least ideally. To Brian, it very much felt as if he was sending a message in a bottle and was hoping it would return to his shore with the answer he was seeking.

***

On Monday afternoon, Ismet called Brian into her office regarding Arnold Fechner, a recent recipient whom Brian had approved for deliveries:

"Brian, his meals are coming back undelivered because he isn't there."

"Well,…I don't know what to say, Ismet. When I met with him and his son two weeks ago, the son said that he was housebound."

"And what did Mr. Fechner say?"

"He… I mean, he claimed that he went out sometimes, but his son assured me that this was just in his mind."

"Why didn't you take Mr. Fechner's word for it, if he said that?"

"Because… Ismet, you know as well as I that a lot of these people aren't capable of making these decisions for themselves. His son assured me that he would be home. He's his Power-of-Attorney."

"Even so, we've had this discussion before, Brian."

"Ismet, I approved him because I believed he met the criteria."

"You believe *everyone*, and that's the problem. Tim and Shanda don't approve at nearly the rate that you do."

Brian needed to pause, because his instinct was to question their standards. "Ismet, I can't speak for them. I can only speak for who's in front of me at these interviews. I go by what I hear and what I see, and I feel that I'm – "

"Brian, I asked you to exercise greater discipline with these applicants."

"And I feel I have."

"Well, here I am with not just Mr. Fechner but five new names in front of me who are reportedly out when deliveries come. We have staff that we pay during the week to make these deliveries and it's a waste of our money and their footsteps."

"Ismet, I'm sorry, but…I don't know what to tell you, unless…you're…you're pretty much telling me to be quicker to reject these people."

Ismet took this in, and as she did, Brian could sense that her tolerance was being tested. "Brian, I'm not saying to reject people for the sake of rejecting them."

"No, I understand that – "

"But what I *am* saying is that, if I go back several months, I see that your percentage of acceptances of people who've proven to be at least somewhat unreliable hasn't diminished – and it's troubling considering that we've had this conversation before."

"Ismet, I really think - "

"Brian, please. Now I need you to update their status and we're going to cease deliveries until their circumstances change."

He slowly rose, motioned towards the door, before turning back to her. "Well, how will you know?"

She paused. "What do you mean?"

"Well, I mean, they could be lying the next time someone goes there, right?"

She grinned unpleasantly at this. "We'll give them the benefit of the doubt."

He nodded, then as if it was a thought that he didn't intend to be heard, "Or maybe you'll just send Tim or Shanda."

Ismet appeared genuinely surprised at his audacity, but said nothing, as Brian left.

Brian thought he could come into this meeting without a compulsion to be defensive. He'd at least become good at not seizing an opportunity to be such, aided by his self-imposed teachings, but there was something unnerving about his continually being portrayed as the weak link among the three case workers when, in fact, he was giving so much of himself to the position. He still wasn't reporting the overtime he was working. He had kept to himself well enough since his exchange with Tim. He tried to appease Ismet and did not feel deceitful in his practice of approving most of the applicants,…but he ultimately could not find it anything other than inane to think that the same people Ismet was rejecting would be reconsidered in the future, especially if Brian was the one assessing them. And what was ultimately insulting was it being portrayed to Brian that he was costing them money, and Tim and Shanda were somehow the fiscal heroes, even if their more judicious approaches were attributed more to their laziness than anything commendable.

He had no desire to follow up his comment about his co-workers with an apology or an explanation. At this point, if Ismet did not see or wish to address their apathy, it now clearly shed light on her own administrative deficiencies. He simply returned to his desk.

After he revised the status of Arnold Fechner to "Currently Ineligible", he would scroll down to the next name Ismet gave. But before he reached it, he noticed that Gwendolyn Fochetti's name was colored red; the red color indicating that a recipient was no longer receiving deliveries. He saw that the change was made within the last hour, with no other details noted. He immediately felt a shiver through him and an odd queasiness, telling him that something was horribly wrong.

"Who revised Fochetti?!" he asked suddenly to the air. Only Shanda was in the office, and his question did nothing to alter her data entry and the pulsating dance club in her ears. Brian stood up to notice Tim's absence, before walking to Shanda's desk, "Shanda?"

She still didn't reply, until she saw Brian approaching. He pointed to his ears, "Can you please turn that off for a second, Shanda?"

She slowly pressed stop on her phone, looked at him curiously, "Yes?"

"Shanda, did you revise Fochetti?"

"What?"

"Fochetti. Gwendolyn Fochetti. She's a recipient."

"Okay, what about her?"

"She's marked as no longer receiving deliveries. I just delivered to her on Saturday."

"I didn't note anything on her. Maybe it was Tim."

"Well, where is he?"

"He's doing assessments."

He looked at Tim's empty chair, and spoke to himself. "It's gotta' be a mistake."

"What?" she asked, without interest.

"I said it's gotta' be a mistake."

"Maybe somethin' happened," she said, apathetically, as she looked at her screen...

"I just saw her Saturday. I just... She was fine. I don't see how this change could've been made just a couple of days later."

"I dunno' what to tell ya'. Ask Ismet."

Brian felt odd going back in there after ending his recent exchange with Ismet somewhat hostilely, but in actuality she was the best source of such information. He knocked on her door.

"Yes?"

Brian entered. "Ismet, I'm sorry, I have to ask you about a recipient."

"Who?" she asked, with a similar level of indifference as Shanda.

"She's someone I've delivered to on the weekends. She's been getting meals here for years, and I know she wouldn't just cancel or… I mean, I just saw her on Saturday."

"Brian, who are you talking about?"

"Gwendolyn Fochetti. F-O-C-H-E-T – "

"Brian," she cut him off, and as this was recent news, she immediately could connect the name. "I know who she is," as her tone abruptly changed.

"Well, why is she – ?"

"Stan went to her apartment to deliver her meal this morning, but he couldn't go up. There was a fire. I called the building management, and they said the poor woman's apartment went up in flames on Sunday. It was contained on the floor, and it didn't spread to other apartments, thankfully – "

"What happened to her?" Brian asked, with surprising firmness.

Ismet paused, taking full notice of Brian's heightened concern. "Brian, she died."

"Oh no…" he said to himself. "Oh…oh no. No, she…" He stood there, stunned, as Ismet couldn't help but take notice of how he seemed so deeply invested in her well-being, but Brian was no longer cognizant of her being in the same room. "She…she…" his voice began to choke, before he ran out of the office and into the street, as if the fire was still occurring.

He hobbled the twelve blocks to Ms. Fochetti's building as fast as he could, arriving out of breath and sweating profusely, though his emotions denied all of it. His instinct was to go to the entry to the building, but he stopped, immediately smelling the ash in the air left over from the previous day. He walked back down the eroding concrete steps and looked up to the 4th floor and could see the blackened bricks surrounding where Ms. Fochetti's living room window was, now boarded up:

"You da' son?!"

Brian barely came out of his emotional trance at the site of Ms. Fochetti's former home and looked at where this grating question in broken English was coming from. At the steps of the entrance was an Asian man of no more than five feet, in a short sleeve flannel shirt and jeans that appeared to be worn daily for years. "I'm sorry?" Brian weakly asked him.

"You da' son? Fochetti's?"

"Uh… No, I… No. I'm…I'm a friend," his words faded, as he looked back up at the blown-out window.

"I'm the supa'. You not da' son?"

"No, I'm not her son," he emphasized, while still gazing up.

"She died, you know. The flames, burn 'er up. Everything in there."

Hearing these words from this stranger was even worse than hearing them from Ismet. From Ismet, there was at least a certain tonal sensitivity in her relaying the news, since she sensed Brian cared for her on a personal level. But to hear that she was burned up from this crude runt who may've not been comfortable enough with English to phrase it more delicately was like an injury to himself. But it was the truth. And, in the end, the truth needed to be accepted, even if it pained Brian. Death was part of life. And perhaps wherever she was now was better than the life she was living, at least her last years. She wasn't impaired mentally in a way where she imagined she was somewhere else leading a different type of existence. She knew that she was biding time, as it were. She knew she was likely being ignored by her kids. She knew that watching talk shows and living among the paper ruins of old catalogues was a crutch of sorts, even if she acted as if they were essential.

All he could think about were the times he went into that apartment over the last year on Saturdays. He now rued how it took so long for him to offer his assistance to her in cleaning up her apartment, or not taking some initiative in getting her some assistance. He could've sought out this super, wherever he lived, and asked him to help her clean out at least some of the many flammable items that, in hindsight, appeared to be waiting to be ignited. Maybe if the super knew how she was living, she would be forced to let them throw some if not all of it away, and thus she'd be alive. But he did nothing.

"Don't know how to reach them?" the man blared.

"Wha…who?" Brian asked, still in a daze.

"Da' son. I know she had a son. A daughta'. But no numba' for them. No contact info."

"Yeah, she… She didn't speak to them a lot. But they should know."

"Leave it to the cops. It's done. Sad, though. Nice lady. Weird lady, but nice."

He tried to hold it together, as he remained looking up at the burnt-out window.

He then recalled their last exchange and how tight she hugged him, as if she knew something was going to happen. It was so clearly apparent now. Something compelled him to tell her how much she meant to him before he left, and he was so glad he did. It was the one thing he felt he didn't allow to be restrained in him. He was glad that his inhibitions of making her feel in any way awkward were absent in that moment. He said what he needed to say and what he hoped meant something to her. Her hug, and the strength of it, led him to believe that it did. But he could've done something else, he believed. He couldn't say now that it wouldn't have been worth overriding her protests or risking her feeling violated by having stuff taken out by force, nor could he rest on believing that the fire was fate; a subconscious suicide that Ms. Fochetti was strategizing all along. *Something could've been done, for Godsakes.*

The man turned to re-enter the building, then stopped, "When d'you last see 'er?"

Every question or comment that emanated from this man was like a long-nailed scratch against glass, but Brian didn't have the strength to tactfully shut him up. "Saturday," he exhaled.

"You friend, you say?"

"Yes," he managed, still not looking at him.

"Sad. Weird lady, but nice. All burned up," he repeated to the air, as if he had said the same thing to tenants and passersby who may or may not have cared to inquire. Then he followed, "Only da' cat."

At this, Brian turned to him, assured that he misheard: "What?"

The super was surprised that Brian was now looking at him, "What, what?"

"You said something about the cat?"

"Oh, yeah. One cat survive, you believe it? Fireman said they were gonna' bring 'im to shelter, but he ain't gonna' get adopted. Tree legs, hair all fucked up. No way, poor thing."

"Socrates," Brian mumbled to himself.

"What?"

"His name is Socrates."

"Really? I didn't know. Like da' Greek guy, right?"

"Yeah. Philosopher," Brian again mumbled, as if not consciously aware he was responding, but nevertheless stunned that the cat managed to survive. He recalled Ms. Fochetti's very recent story about how she found him, and in the moment was at least glad he managed to ask about Socrates before it was too late. It gave another window into the kind of person she was and, considering the plight that Socrates had endured, what kind of cat he was. When recalling this, he could not help but admire the remarkable stubbornness this cat had, that despite his physical defects, his will to live appeared to be absurdly strong. And yet he could only marvel why. Was the cat so blindly committed to enduring more of this life, in whatever pain he was now in? Didn't he know the woman who saved him from the trash was gone? If what the super said was true, Socrates must have only wondered what he had done to deserve all that he had gone through – and to not even have the luxury of an expeditious death, but to linger in a shelter among other abandoned animals who could have only looked more appealing than this three-legged feline freak of nature.

"Do you know where the shelter is?"

"Da' what?"

"The animal shelter. You said the firemen brought the cat to a shelter."

"Yeah, but I don't know where. You can ask dem. Fire department's a few blocks down Broadway."

He looked back up at the boarded window and the blackened bricks that surrounded it, wondering if he'd ever have occasion to be on this block again, since there were no other deliveries in the immediate area. That could change, of course. But as far as Brian was concerned, he hoped to never have a reason to look at the building again. It was now another block he would avoid.

He came upon the nearest fire department, Ladder 17 at East 143rd Street. There was only one man around, a short, burly fellow with a buzzcut and mustache, sipping a Diet Coke and dragging a cigarette in the garage. "Hi, I have a question, sir," as Brian approached.

The man looked at Brian strangely, as if he was about to be solicited.

"A friend of mine died in a fire on Sunday, on 137th Street. She had a cat. The super said it was rescued. I was jus' curious where he is."

"Where who is? The cat?" the man finally uttered.

"Yeah."

"I dunno'. Wasn't on that one. Who told you dey took a cat?" as if they were being accused of theft.

"The super in the building. He said the cat survived and they took him to a shelter."

"Then maybe he's at the shelter. I dunno'," he inhaled his cigarette.

"Well, do you know *which* shelter? I don't know where the nearest shelter is around here."

It seemed all this man could do to even recall, before "There's one…I think, on 115th. Sometimes we take 'em there. I forget da' name. You sure he said dey took the cat?"

"Yeah, he was pretty sure. It's pretty distinct, too. It's a tabby, it has three legs. I don't know what condition he was in after the fire, but that's all I have. His name is Socrates."

"I dunno', I didn't see any cats when I came in today, three or four legs, aside from Turbo, who lives here. He takes care a' the mice. I'd check the nearest shelter'n see what they say," he swigged the rest of his soda, his interest in this topic having not increased in the slightest.

"Well, look, um, could I...?" Brian wondered if it was worth bothering. The apathetic vibe he was getting from this man was not unlike the apathy he felt from Tim and Shanda. And what did he intend to do, after all? He had no intentions of keeping the cat himself, with his voracious dander allergies alongside a complete lack of desire to have a pet. In the end, it just didn't seem right to him that the cat should be in limbo and so he at least wanted assurance that Socrates would either have a home or, if his health situation was dire, that he would be put down humanely. There was something about being assured of his status that helped soften the blow of Ms. Fochetti's sudden death.

"Look, could I give you my name and number and when some of your crew get back, maybe you could ask them and maybe someone can call me and just let me know where he is?"

"Alright," the man said. "You got a card?"

"Uh, no, I just… Can I send you my info?"

"How ya' gonna' do that?"

"Well, if you give me your number, I can text you…"

"Nah, nah, nah, nah. I don't give that out. C'mere."

The obviously put-out man led Brian to the back office where Brian wrote his information down on a post-it note, then handed it to him. "Your name is…?"

"Lou," he managed.

"Okay, thanks, Lou."

"So, what, you wana' adopt it or what?"

At this, Brian paused. First, surprised that Lou even exhibited enough interest to ask, but that was quickly replaced by his own uncertainty as to what he would really do if anyone would call. At this point, he didn't assume they would. They were New York City firemen, known for their heroism but by no means their bedside manner. They were busy, especially now that it was summer. No one would ever call.

"Uh, yeah," Brian lied. Then left.

Fourteen

—

Outside the fire department, he did a quick search of local shelters on his phone and found only one roughly twenty blocks away. He called and described Socrates, assuming that his three limbs would be distinctive enough for them, to which the person on the line said that there were no such cats brought in since Sunday. At that point, Brian felt he did as much as he could do. He knew Socrates was likely not long for the world, and his efforts in finding him appeared to be as much as could be reasonably asked for. He had went to the fire department, gave his information, called the nearest shelter – and there was no sign of him.

He remained on the corner and, to Brian, it felt as if he was at an intersection that was more symbolic of his life than the city itself. He had to go back to the office, but he wondered what he was going back to. From there, he would go home – but, again, what was he going back to? He put in his earphones, hit play, and Jeff Gammon's dulcet delivery would bring him back to center, as his words again made the hot city blocks and the many aimlessly walking more tolerable:

"Life is fleeting. We've heard it. We know of its brevity. But how we act within the sliver of time that we have is what can make our lives substantial, regardless of its length. That's what we have control over. You have control over this. You are never at the mercy of a bad situation, even if it seems that there is nothing that you can do. There is always something. There is always...something."

He saw Jakween for what seemed like the first time in a while. When he was there, he received the food Brian brought as if it were the grandest gesture, "Tank you, my friend. Diss is beautiful."

"I hope you like eggplant parmigiana," Brian weakly smiled.

"Of course! You bring, I eat. I'm easy. But I love eggplant. Very nice of you."

Brian had somehow hoped this would be one of the days where Jakween was elsewhere and could just hide the food in his cardboard abode. It didn't dawn on him until he saw him that he hadn't smiled for a while, and the news of Ms. Fochetti, in addition to what was becoming a progressively depressing work environment, was weighing on him.

"Enjoy, Jakween. Let me know how it is," Brian followed, as he started to walk away.

"You okay, my friend?" Jakween asked, as he always did.

Brian felt that it was an insult to Jakween to be in motion, and abruptly stopped to answer him. "Oh, I'm…I'm good, Jakween. Just a little tired."

"You work hard, I know. Well, get some rest, my friend. Tank you."

Brian took a moment to appreciate Jakween's sentiment, and managed to summon "You too, my friend. Always good to see you," before he left. On the walk to his apartment building, he wondered how long he had ignored Jakween prior to hearing of the death of Leslie Scanlon. He was ashamed to remember how he had come to look at homeless people as part of the architecture of the city, not unlike the pigeons that ambled about and defecated at will. How long was he living near the vacant pharmacy before he finally noticed him and felt obligated to feed him? *What happened to him?* And yet, he seemed so happy and of sound mind. He seemed more appreciative of the world than the people he worked with and most who he had come in contact with. And then, just as he became too admiring of Jakween, he wondered if he had done anything he was ashamed of. Was his current situation a punishment or atonement for something?

By the time he got home, he noticed a text had come from a number he didn't recognize. He opened it, then read:

> *Hey, Brian*
> *Got your note. I'm good to meet up after 5 tomorrow, if that works. I'll have about an hour.*
> *Let me know.*
> *Chad*

Brian needed to read it over several times before fully absorbing that what he had set in motion was about to come to fruition. He analyzed where Chad could be coming from, tone not being particularly obvious in texts. He wasn't sure if Chad would know what this would be about. Could he really think he was going to meet Brian for coffee and catch up on baseball? Would Chad be upset with Brian for his sudden social introversion? Nothing could be known for sure, except that they would soon be meeting.

"How 'bout those Mets?" Chad rhetorically asked, with a weak snicker, as he shook Brian's hand. To Brian's unsettlement, Chad was already at a table dead center of the café floor, and since it was rush hour, there was no shortage of traffic coming in and out.

"Hey, right?" Brian awkwardly agreed, before reluctantly sitting. In his mind, he quickly realized that this was poor planning. He should've offered a more off-peak time to speak, but felt strange in being too specific. He looked around at the patrons entering and exiting.

"You okay?" Chad asked.

"Yeah, uh,…yeah. It's just busier than I expected."

"Everyone's jus' gettin' off," Chad noted, as if surprised that Brian would expect anything else.

"Yeah, I know. I should've taken that into… I never come in here, really. I just thought it'd be a good place to…" Suddenly, he saw a table open up in the corner, dimly lit and somewhat removed from the rest of the tables. "Chad, I'm sorry. Do you mind if we grab that table?"

Chad looked at what Brian was pointing to, then came back to him, strangely. "Sure, uh…yeah." Chad took the iced latte he had already purchased in his hand and followed Brian, who rushed to the table before it could be claimed by someone else. They both sat.

"This okay?" Chad chuckled.

"Oh, yeah. Much better. Thanks for your indulgence."

"Nah, it's fine. S'how're things?"

"Uh,…y'know, pretty busy. Juggling some things."

"You still in security?" Chad remembered.

"Oh, wow. You… No, I left that a while ago. I'm working for a not-for-profit. Food-on-Feet. Have you ever…?"

"Oh, yeah. The food delivery for seniors'n…?"

"Yeah. And housebound. Yeah."

"Interesting," Chad nodded, then sipped his latte. "Why'd y'change?"

"Well, it was… I just wanted to do something that felt a little more meaningful to me, I guess. I'd been in security a while'n I guess I sort of hit the wall with it, a bit."

"Yeah, I hear that. Good f'you, man," he sipped again.

At this point, Brian wondered how much of a ramp of small talk he should give their meeting before revealing his ultimate purpose. Chad didn't appear particularly curious as to why Brian reached out to him after such a long time, and that made it all the more troubling for Brian in terms of how he should broach his intended topic.

"Yeah, it… Thank you. You? How're you doing? The family?" Brian inquired with forced enthusiasm.

"Oh, they're good, thanks. Sherry's gettin' big."

"That's…your daughter?"

"Yeah. God, it's surreal."

"How old now?"

"Seven."

"Wow."

"Yep, she's somethin'," he sipped again.

"That's awesome. Congrats."

"Thanks. You gonna' get somethin', or…?"

"Oh, I'm… I'll wait on that. Uh, listen, I know you're busy with your work and family'n all, and so I appreciate you being willing to meet. I know it may be a little weird."

Chad took a moment, then smiled. "In what way?"

"Well, y'know, we haven't really…spoken like this. We haven't really said much in a while, and so I know this must seem…"

"What?"

"Well, just…odd. Right?" Brian nervously chuckled, surprised in that it appeared that it didn't seem to particularly phase Chad.

"Yeah, I guess. I didn't really think much of it. I figure you've had stuff goin' on. Hey, stuff happens. I get it. We're workin' hard, y'know? No judgment here," he smiled, then took another swig. At this, Brian felt even further removed from where he wanted to go with their discussion. It wasn't like he sculpted a speech that he would say or, for that matter, was after a particular solution to anything. Ultimately, it was just a burning need to discuss what had heretofore been the undiscussable with anyone. He was tired of being vague, but there was no one to go into specifics with other than someone whom he knew witnessed the exact same thing as he did. This would have to amount to something, in his mind.

After Chad spoke, Brian had no further resources to delve into as far as air-filling conversation, and not even a beverage to sip to offset the awkwardness, and so he could only smile at him, before looking around to assure that no one was too close. His voice then lowered, as he carefully leaned in: "Chad, look, um…there's… There's a real reason why I suddenly stopped…engaging in conversation in the lobby, like we used to sometimes. I know we used to talk about the Mets and the Knicks and the Jets, but…I have to be honest, I don't have a clue how any of them are doing."

Chad's eyes suddenly had a curiousness to them. "Okay."

Brian took a moment, then "Did you know that Randy Scanlon is gonna' be released in a couple of weeks?"

Chad absorbed this, as if trying to recall. "Randy…? Who's that?"

Brian was stunned. He didn't know how Chad was absorbing the incident this whole time, but at least expected the name of the assailant would have relevance to him. "Who is it? The guy we saw beat his wife to death, between 35th and 36th avenue. Over a year'n a half ago. She was in a coma, then she died."

After a moment, Chad's face moved to one of recognition without any attachment beyond it. "Okay, yeah. I remember. I didn't know he was gettin' out. Shit. How long did he serve?"

"18 months."

"Jeez, that's it?"

Brian took another moment, disappointed in Chad's lack of knowledge. "Yeah, that's it. His father's a judge or something, so I'm sure that had something to do with it. Who knows? But, yeah, he's getting out."

Chad mulled this over. "Wow," then sipped his latte. "Didn't know."

"Man, I thought *I* avoided the news," Brian weakly snickered.

"Well, I'm busy, man. I'm working two jobs. I barely have time for *this*," he chuckled, then sipped again. "So is that what you wanted to talk to me about?"

"Well,…yeah."

"Okay, well,…thanks for lettin' me know," Chad sat there, wondering if this was how the discussion would end.

"I mean, that's *not* it, Chad. I didn't think it'd be news to you, really. But that wasn't the main thing I wanted to talk about here."

At this point, Chad became a bit cautious, and in his caution Brian could feel the clock ticking as to how much time he would have with him. He couldn't read exactly why Chad would feel this way, or if he was feeling cornered. Brian knew from his confrontation with Tim at the office weeks ago that it was challenging to confront someone, however delicately, about something they may be ashamed or defensive of. In the moment, he desperately was trying to learn from it.

"Chad, we watched that man…" he took a breath, "we watched that man beat his ex-wife, Leslie, and we didn't…" his voice started to choke, "we didn't do anything."

And then it was clear. Chad removed his hand from his sweating iced latte, and sat back in his chair with his arms now crossed. Brian did not need to be a detective or psychologist to know that this was a pose of some resistance. "Brian, what is this?" his voice now significantly lower and restrained, as his eyes locked into Brian's.

Brian was nervous, but there was no benefit for him to go this far only to let Chad off the hook. He looked around again, pulled his chair in closer towards the small café table, "Chad, I have to…", he paused, then took a breath. "Look, this has been with me. It's been with me and I've tried to… Everything I'm doing in my life now is because of what I saw that evening. Okay?"

"Okay," Chad said, as if awaiting the other shoe.

"I'm not at my old job because of what happened. Everything I'm doing in my life now, it's all because I've been trying to, I guess,…make amends for what I didn't do, and there's been no one I can talk to about it and I thought I was…I was hiding it well enough, until I heard he was getting out. And I guess in finding that out, it's like the whole thing just happened yesterday and I can't hide from it anymore. D'you understand?"

Chad took a moment. "Yeah, but I don't understand why you're telling *me*, Brian."

Brian took this in, trying to suppress his frustration that Chad was numb to his intent. "There's only so many people I can talk to about this. There's almost nobody, actually. You're really the only one."

"The only one?"

"Yes!"

"Look, with all due respect, we hardly know each other, man."

"About *this*! You're the only one I can talk to about *this*, okay?"

"Why?" he came in closer, though it appeared he would leap up and out of the café at any moment.

"Because we were there."

Chad swallowed. "Other people were there too."

"But I didn't see them. I didn't notice them. We were standing next to each other coming out of the train. You're the only one I know for a fact was there, Chad. And we need to talk about this."

"Talk about what, Brian? I don't know what – "

"This man is gonna' walk free and I'm sick over it. But I feel just as responsible as him, okay? We all should."

"Hey, look, man,…this is a free country. You can feel however you wana' feel, Brian. But don't rope me into whatever you're puttin' yourself through, okay?"

"Don't you feel terrible?"

"Brian, look – "

"Don't you wish you at least called the cops?"

"Someone did."

"But not us."

"There was like a dozen people around, Brian. How many calls need to be made for the same crime?"

"911 said one call came in from a neighboring building, from someone who saw it outa' there window."

"You don't know that."

"It was on the news after it happened."

"Alright, fine. Still, someone called."

"And by then it was too late, Chad. Don't you see? Everyone that was standing in the street that night just watched. The only phones that were out were filming it. We were all fucking useless. Don't you remember?"

"Brian, look – "

"We just stood there like statues and watched like it was on pay-per-view and did nothing while this guy beat the hell out of his ex-wife in the street – "

Suddenly, Chad leaned in closer, "Brian, dial it down, okay?" he said in a sudden hushed whisper, barely on the fringe of decorum, as he looked around at the few eyes glancing over.

Brian halted, aware that his volume was rising, as he too couldn't help but notice their surroundings. He took a breath, then came back to Chad. "Don't you think about it?"

"No, I don't."

Brian leaned in further, looked at Chad's latte on the table, then softly: "Is it your family?"

"What?" he asked sharply.

"Do they know you were there?"

Chad's face suddenly tightened, as if Brian's question brought him to a next level of insult.

"What do you care what they know?"

"Chad, I'm just – "

"What, are you gonna' try and blackmail me or somethin'?"

"What? No, Chad, that's not…that's not at all what this is about."

"Then what the fuck d'you care what they know? They knew it happened. Crimes happen every other minute in this city. All they care about is that I'm not part of 'em."

"But you *were* a part of this one. We were all part of it."

Chad suddenly dropped his hands on the table, and sharply rasped, "Are you insane, man? We saw some jacked-up steroid-addict beat a woman in a fucking rage, and *he's* responsible. No one else. He's the only one. I work two fuckin' jobs to support my family, n'I'm not gonna' throw myself in the ring with some nutcase'n get myself killed so that they have no one to support 'em. I have a stake. What's *your* stake? Huh? You have a wife?"

"No, but – "

"You have a kid?"

"Chad,…"

"No. So what was *your* excuse? Ask yourself that? Forget about everyone else. Why didn't *you* do somethin'?"

Brian was paralyzed, and knew there was nothing left to say – and so he said it. But he knew the answer. He did nothing because he was afraid, and it was his fear that made it easy to align with everyone else who likely felt the same or even looked at the incident as an entertainment cheaper than cable. Chad seemed to feel a sense of victory in shutting Brian up, but he was too angry to gloat, as he slowly leaned back into his chair, grabbed his latte, which he now had nothing but distaste for, and left.

If there was a victory in any of this, it was that for as long as Brian lived in that building, there would be no ambiguity between he and Chad. A line was drawn. There was no longer the slightest possibility of friendship. There was no longer a neighborly obligation to say a word to each other, despite the proximity of their mailboxes. They were simply two people who lived in the same building, who would have nothing to do with each other.

In the end, the ultimate purpose of this meeting was for Brian to feel that he was not alone in his guilt. But he was. He knew that now. The indistinguishable faces that were near them during the incident were vaporous in their importance. Chad was the only one whom he recalled. The only one whose feelings mattered on this to Brian. And now that he knew that

Chad held no responsibility for his inaction, it all but cemented the feeling that Brian felt all along but was trying so desperately to inter – that he was responsible. What was worse was that Chad was right. What *was* Brian's stake? He had nothing in his life, at that point. No family, a couple of hangout buddies, a relationship with Sara that teetered on nothingness. A belief in nothing. A tenuous connection to his father and sister. If there was anyone who should've found it within to overcome their fear and throw themself in front of Randy Scanlon, it was Brian.

What did he have to lose?

Fifteen

The ensuing days were a morose blur. Brian went into the office dutifully enough, entered data for part of the day, had a few field assessments with potential recipients, but there was a detachment that had not been there before. Suddenly, his existence felt as mechanical as it had when he numbly stood alongside a revolving door as a security guard. With the ulcerating residue from his failed meeting with Chad, combined with Ms. Fochetti's death and Randy Scanlon's forthcoming release, he felt all the more that there was nothing special to what he was doing. If not him, it'd be someone else in his position; perhaps caring less, but more-or-less incurring the same results. He was becoming too despondent to even volunteer at the suicide hotline. How could he?, he thought. If he was no good to himself, what good could he be to someone else grasping for a justification for living? Even the *I Ching* noted that one should never offer wisdom who can't inhabit such wisdom themselves.

He tried reading excerpts from some of his favorite spiritual-based books by the Dalai Llama, Deepak

Chopra and others, but his attention wasn't there. It may as well've been braille. The fail-safe was always Jeff Gammon's voice. He could pick a random chapter from the audiobook and usually it'd have relevance to what he needed on that day.

When he arrived home on Friday evening, after dropping off Jakween's meal, he wanted to do nothing else but immerse himself in his couch and tune out the world as best he could. He closed his eyes, and in his ears Gammon spoke:

"Never be afraid to be kind. There is a tendency now in our skeptical world to think that those who are kind to us have an ulterior motive. They can't simply be kind for kind's sake. They have to want something. And in that assumption, we become defensive. And it is that defensiveness that then creates a rift – a chasm between our desire to be kind and one's desire to receive that kindness for what it is. And so what happens? If we are the latter, then we resign that, unless we know someone well, they must be dubious in their intent. And if we're the former, we can become afraid to be kind for fear of making people uncomfortable. And so what's the solution here? To not be afraid. To not be afraid to be kind or to receive that kindness. Because fear is the albatross. Fear is the cancer of a society. If we live fear-based, we live warily. We live without a sense of love. Without a sense of hope. Without a sense of being a part of the greater

good. We only live for our own comfort. Where's the victory in that?"

He hit stop, and tried to absorb the words and decipher if he'd gone about everything wrong in the new incarnation of his life. Aside from Jakween getting free meals, and the people he had pleasant exchanges with when delivering food or at the suicide hotline, or the charity events he partook in, it now seemed to Brian that he simply might not be very good at being good. Or much of anything else. When musing over who was in his life that meant anything to him, he was barren. What had he done? Why had he wiped the slate so clean after he quit his security job? Was it really necessary to stop returning Lucas's calls? To break up with Sara? The lack of substance of his past relationships all of a sudden seemed more significant than what was there now.

He looked at his phone to notice the pending message that he had never listened to from Vanessa, that had been sitting there on the verge of being permanently erased from his voicemail. He decided there was no better time than now to listen to it:

"Hey, Brian - It's Vanessa. Just wanted to check in and see how the leg's doing. I hope you're doing okay. I really enjoyed our lunch. Sorry if I was a little too…I dunno, whatever. (she snickered) I have that tendency to be too whatever sometimes, but, in any case, just

wanted to say hi. You have my number, so feel free to buzz me, if you want. No worries either way. I work until 4 during the week, just so you know. Take care, okay?"

It pleased him to hear her voice and her energy simply because she was not tethered to anything else in his life. She was simply someone who fell out of the sky and was kind, just like Jeff Gammon had noted in the very segment he had just heard. And yes, Brian did recall how suspicious he was the first time she approached him at the walkathon, and rued at his skepticism.

Out of his feeling of regret, then came his memory of their lunch and the many topics they discussed; life's meaning, spirituality, death. He realized that he had never had such a conversation with someone before and, while it enlivened his senses to a degree he had not experienced purely on an intellectual level, it also shed light on how little he still knew. Vanessa appeared to be in-process as well, as an admittedly half-assed Buddhist practitioner, but he could only admire her fearlessness. He didn't even know what she did for a living, and yet it didn't appear to matter. He also didn't give particular thought to her as a modestly attractive woman, which she was. But his libido was in an attic, of little importance to him. The stimulus was her questions and responses, and Brian fielding them like tennis balls that could bounce to him from any direction. She appeared to not be particularly interested in him romantically either, and maybe that was also refreshing. She just seemed to care. But that also scared him. She was in the know of the world more than he. And it was that that led to his resistance in calling her, particularly her noting of past accusations against Gammon. He never bothered to follow up and investigate this because just the possibility of it being true would then call into question much of what had become his life's philosophy. And it would now be even more damaging in light of his encounter with Chad and the death of Ms. Fochetti, and the seeming tenuousness by which he held his job. He felt so much more unstable since their lunch, and so it didn't feel he had any logical footing in responding to her. In the end, she would ask questions, more out of curiosity than invasiveness, but it wouldn't be any easier for him. And what if she brought up recent news of his mentor?

It couldn't be true.

He didn't dream much, because he now wasn't sleeping much. Every time he closed his eyes, he simply hoped that he could fall into a blissful siesta for just a few hours, which would wake him to his alarm rested, refreshed, and lucid. And with it would come an optimism that he was rapidly losing sight of. He felt now that if he could just get a few hours of solid sleep and tune recent events out as best he could, somehow he would come back to a place of at least feeling that he was more of a contributor to the greater good than one of millions of lost souls. But he deduced that he was so much more lost than most, now. How many people could say they stood fifty feet from a crime and did nothing but remain encased in their own fear? In the ensuing months from the incident, he did in fact read about the Bystander Effect, which all but confirmed what had happened on that evening. That a person tends to conform to a group dynamic, especially when witnessing someone being victimized, which is why so often there are crimes committed with eyewitnesses that are never interfered with. And yet, if one person took it upon themselves to take action, the likelihood that others would follow suit was also quite common. *Why couldn't I be that one?*, he asked. And he still did. He asked it so many times until he began laying building blocks atop such ruminations. And in his efforts to give back, and improve his life by helping the lives of others, he had hoped the question would be well-submerged – but it was always close to the surface. It was why he couldn't get too close to anyone. Why being at all revealing with someone, like he became with Ms. Fochetti, often rendered him on the verge of an emotional geyser. He felt somehow that she always knew his life was a sort of penance for past sins, and yet she seemed to admire him so. And now she was gone.

Perhaps gone to the same place that Leslie Scanlon resided – perhaps Heaven. Or somewhere else. And then he wondered if they saw the light that Vanessa claimed to see, from her near-death experience. Could he put any solace in that? Or was it really just darkness that lay ahead?

He woke up feeling terrible. To compound it further, it was Saturday morning, and the first in which he'd likely be delivering to the same route that Ms. Fochetti was on since her passing. There was no way he could do it. There was even no way he could scroll through the *F*s in the database and not feel sickened to see her name in red. He sent an email to Tim and Shanda and told them he had the flu. He at least had sick days, which he had never used, and there didn't appear to be a better time to use them. Then just as he despaired as to what he would do with his day, other than hole himself up in his apartment, he realized the significance of it being Saturday by the early morning sounds of children in the playground. He looked out the window, then looked at the clock on the wall and saw it was just after eight – as early as he was up last week when he saw the man with the fedora enter alone, which seemed to all but confirm a nefarious motive. His heart started to beat as he approached his window and looked down at the park. The parents and children were beginning to gather, as the morning would be the coolest part of what was forecasted to be an oppressively humid day. In would trickle a mother with a son, a mother with a daughter, a father with twins… As he waited, he was overcome with a feeling of just what these relationships would amount to as these kids got older. Their parents were so attentive now, but at what point would that end – at what point would apathy intervene or a strain in a marriage show its face, averting its eyes from the offspring – which was all that Brian seemed to remember. At least his sister Kim could learn from it with their kids. That is unless she and her husband were somehow fated to re-peat the actions of their parents. *But, my God*, he thought, *at the very least these kids deserve to be safe. At the very –*

And then he saw the man, alone, with the book bag and fedora stroll in unassumingly as he approached his favorite bench: "Not on my watch", Brian tremblingly mumbled, before he blasted out the door as if pushed by a herculean force that would not even allow him to pause. It seemed to take him seconds to get from his apartment on the fourth floor to the hot pavement out-side of his building, as he wrapped around the corner, his peripheral vision all but non-existent, before mak-ing his way to the entrance to the playground. He stopped, looked at the parents with their kids – several now on the jungle gym, or heading down the slide, then turned sharply to see the man, looking older and thinner than he seemed from a distance, whose book was out – what looked like the same tattered paper-back the man had had in his hands for weeks; *a ruse,*

Brian thought, without question. His look became a stare which launched knives into this man, but that wouldn't be enough. He was this far now, and there was no turning back. He had to do something. He had to save these children from this fedora-donned pedophile just waiting for the chance to whisk one of them into some dark basement apartment he kept nearby. "Not on my watch," Brian mumbled again. "Not on my Goddamn watch, you sonofabitch!" he then yelled, as a few nearby parents and children looked at him, now startled, before Brian marched towards the man: "HEY!"

The man lowered his book, obviously stunned, as Brian was now standing within inches of the man's crossed pale legs. The man looked at Brian nervously, as Brian needed to catch his breath – his adrenaline beyond what he had ever felt, as if it was percolating and couldn't be turned off without the conclusion of a violent act. He tried to slow his breathing, before summoning enough control to lower his voice to an unusually intense growl: "What are you doing here, sir?"

The man looked around at the suddenly staring eyes, which were looking more at Brian than at him, "What…? I'm sorry, are you…?" he nervously asked.

"Why are you here?! This is a children's playground!" Brian asserted.

"I'm… I'm not understanding – "

"THIS IS A CHILDREN'S PLAYGROUND, SIR! WHY ARE YOU HERE?!"

"Why'm I – ?"

"WHY ARE YOU HERE?!!!"

The man dropped his book at Brian's volume, as he looked around for some sort of assistance from the unsettled eyes around them. "You're leaving!", as Brian yanked the man's arm with a strength that did not appear to be his own. The man's butt slid awkwardly against the smooth wooden bench, as Brian continued to force the man upright… "Get up right now!" as the ambient sounds of shock emerged like waves.

"I don't know what you're – !"

"I SAID GET THE HELL UP, YOU SONOFABITCH! YOU DON'T BELONG HERE!" as the strength of Brian's pull forced the man off the bench and onto the pavement.

Suddenly Brian felt a tug on his arm, "Sir!" came in a deep but authoritative voice. Brian turned sharply, thinking that it must've been a parent that misunderstood the situation, but it was a policeman, backed up by a female officer of similar proportion. Both appeared ready to remove Brian from the playground. "Sir, come with me, please," as the officer tugged on Brian's arm. But Brian was fearless in his defiance, and yanked his arm away.

"Officer, this man shouldn't be here!" as Brian pointed to the man still on the ground, who remained dumbfounded at what was taking place.

"I think *you* shouldn't be here, sir. Please, there're kids here – "

"I know there are kids here, officer. Why do you think *I'm* here?"

"Why *are* you here?" the officer followed.

"I've been watching, okay? I live right in that building. Okay? Right up there, officer! Right in that building – "

"Sir – "

"I've seen this man come and go on Saturdays!"

"Sir, calm down, okay? The man may have right to come in here," the officer speaking to Brian as if he were talking to someone mentally deranged.

"He doesn't have kids! This is a Goddamn children's park, do you understand?! Look at the sign! There's a sign by the entrance that clearly – "

"Sir – " as the officer reached for Brian's arm…

"Look at it, officer! It clearly says that adults must be accompanied by children! Look at it!"

"Sir, I need you – "

"I'M MAKING A CITIZEN'S ARREST!" Brian finally howled, while random heads began popping out of the surrounding apartment windows. "THAT'S WHY I'M HERE! THESE CHILDREN ARE IN DANGER AS LONG AS THIS MAN KEEPS COMING HERE!"

There was a sudden silence and stillness, with only the sounds of Brian's exhausted panting. As he gradually slowed his breathing, he looked around at the eyes upon him: parents frozen with their children. He then looked at the man who remained on the ground looking helplessly at the officers, before Brian's eyes met the nearest one.

"I have grandkids here," a feeble voice managed. It was the man, who slowly rose from the pavement. He spoke pleadingly to the officers, as tears formed in his eyes: "They come with my daughter. We don't speak, but I come to see them. I sit here for an hour, and then I leave. I live just two blocks away, officer. She knows I'm here."

This was a response that Brian didn't expect. He was confused, but still angry. He was determined to believe that this man shouldn't be there. He was lying. What kind of a story was that, to say he was watching grandkids from afar. Brian saw it with his own eyes. He had never seen the man so much as speak or gesture to a soul when he was in the playground. It was a lie, without question.

"Officer, are you gonna' do something?" Brian sharply asked.

"Sir, you may be jumping to conclusions here, okay?" the officer said. "Now – "

"What man comes to a playground by himself unless he has something else on his mind, for Godsakes?!" Brian bellowed.

The officer started to approach Brian. "Sir, I want you to step away from this gentleman and come with us."

"You're not arresting *me* for this!"

"Sir, we'll speak with him, as well. But we want to speak with you outside of the play area so that the children and parents here can go on with their day without being scared."

"Get this man out of here and they won't be!"

The man stood and watched this, evidently afraid to defend himself in front of Brian, who was so clearly enraged and steadfast in his refusal to leave.

"We're scared of *you*!" a young girl's voice emitted, quickly hushed by her parent. Brian turned to the direction of the voice, knowing it was a child, and was instantly humbled. He realized that his emotions had gotten the better of him to the extent that they were likely negating his noble intentions.

The officer extended his hand, in an attempt to lessen any aggressive display in front of the crowd, which had now extended to passersby on the sidewalk. "Sir, please?"

Brian slowly followed the one officer, while the other approached the man in the fedora. As the officer stopped at the corner, just outside of the playground entrance, he looked at Brian who, at this point, was more decompressed and had a semblance of his usual self, despite how he was drenched in sweat and looked unusually unkempt, as he'd just gotten out of bed. "Sir, are you all right?" the officer asked.

"Yes, I'm… I know it looks like I'm… I'm not. I've just been suspicious of that man and – "

"Sir, are you aware that you have no shoes or socks on?" the officer followed.

At this point, Brian looked at his feet, and saw that, in fact, he was barefoot. In his adrenalized state, he couldn't even feel that they were cut up by random rocks and small bits of glass that he must've stepped on as he angrily made his way to the playground.

As the officer observed Brian awestruck at his bloody feet, "Sir, do you have kids?"

"Do…?" Brian looked up at him. "No."

"Why were you in that park?"

"Officer, I've been trying to explain to you. I've been watching from the window on Saturdays and I've seen that man enter the park by himself. I'm sure that he's up to something."

"Why didn't you just call 911 and have someone sent?"

"Because…" Brian couldn't answer this in any way that would make sense to the officer.

"I don't know. I just… It was instinct."

"Instinct."

"I felt that I just had to handle it myself or else nothing would be done."

"We were right around the block, sir."

"Well, I obviously didn't see you, or else I…"

"Regardless, you don't accost people like that, sir. You could be wrong."

"I'm not."

"You heard what he said."

"He's lying. I'm telling you. There's no way…" Out of the corner of his eye, Brian saw the other officer walking away from the mother with her son and daughter, of about 5 or 6. The man with the fedora was dejectedly leaving, already frail-bodied, but significantly weakened by the ordeal, as the mother appeared to watch him depart while her kids looked suitably confused. Brian forgot what he was in the midst of explaining to the officer as he watched this like a depressing silent movie.

"The mother confirmed it. There 'is grandkids," the female officer conveyed to her partner, as if Brian wasn't there. "They live within five blocks of each other, but they're estranged. She knows he comes to the park, but doesn't want anything to do with 'im. The kids don't even know who he is, but they probably do now."

"Tsch, that's messed up," the officer noted.

"Yeah. Didn't get details from her other than that he was a drunk when she was growin' up, but she vouched for 'im. He probably still shouldn't be there, but he's not a predator. Just not much of a father-figure."

Brian looked at the mother through the fence, as she tried to distract her kids back to playing on the jungle gym. His actions now made no sense to him. He wasn't protecting anybody, really. It didn't appear that she wanted her father there, and yet they were his grandchildren. All that Brian managed to do was shed an enormous light on yet another broken family. He was a father who appeared to regret his actions of the past, and a grandfather purely through biology. Perhaps there was some catharsis he was getting in simply being near them in the playground. And maybe his daughter indulged it as long as he didn't approach her or her kids. It was all speculative. But the man in the fedora, in the end, appeared to be nothing more than a man with regrets – not unlike Brian.

The officers escorted the shoeless Brian to his building, wanting to verify that he in fact had a home to go to, since he looked so utterly disturbed in his bed clothes and unkempt hair. What made the journey even more humiliating was that they walked past Jakween who instantly spotted Brian and, even in his state of indigency, could barely contain a baffled expression at seeing the gracious bearer of his freshly nuked meals being escorted by police - and without shoes. *Did he see the whole thing?* Brian wondered. *My God, I didn't think I could ever experience such a humiliating day - and it's not even noon.*

They entered the lobby and, as if it couldn't get more embarrassing for him, there was Chad. And not just Chad, but Chad accompanied by his wife and young daughter, who all unsettlingly watched a disheveled, sweaty and shoeless Brian in T-shirt and flannel pajama bottoms, while bookended by police, as they approached the elevator. The officers would soon enter his apartment with him, conclude that he indeed lived there, before giving him a warning that he was not to enter that playground ever again.

Sixteen

He didn't go to mass on Sunday, nor did he go to confession. As he looked out a different window from his apartment, viewing the less eventful 34th Ave, he simply did not have the wherewithal to do much of anything, and did not see how that would change. Father Devon felt like a very distant presence in his life. The words from his sermons were now as remote as another galaxy. And he didn't know Brian anyway. There was no relationship there. No bond. After seeing the Father escorted into a car a couple of weeks ago to give last rites, it confirmed to Brian that he was relied upon by many – and perhaps, even to a man of such religious allegiance, the many faces who he saw, spoke to and even counseled were indistinguishable. That thought made it all the more apparent to Brian that he was simply a weed among a vast field. *Why even bother going to mass anymore?* He was a sinner, and one of the worst kind. And nothing Father Devon would ever say could change that.

But what encompassed all the philosophies to which Brian committed himself was Jeff Gammon; someone who had heretofore managed to be a reliable vessel from which emerged a sensible way of existing. For Brian, it had been easier to make sense of it all through one source than through a myriad. But the end result of Gammon's teachings for Brian was the mantra that he would find himself chanting in his weakest moments: *My story is not yet written.* Yet now, Brian even questioned *that.* What kind of a story was he writing with his life? Was it really all about altruism? Finding one's bliss? Being kind? He wasn't sure anymore.

The only thing he was certain of in the moment was that he would send an email to Ismet and staff that he was still sick and couldn't come in on Monday. More dire than calling in, he wanted to resign now, as he had come to believe that not only was the work he had done with Food-on-Feet not appreciated, but that he hadn't contributed anything distinctive, despite the kindness and warmth he had tried to display to applicants and recipients. Ms. Fochetti's death seemed to inter all of those pleasant memories and put in the forefront the aligned apathy of Tim and Shanda, and the frustration of Ismet. And then there was that ominous question asked by Delia Warden, whom he had recently approved for deliveries: *"Have you ever done anything that you're ashamed of?",* which Brian was certain now was a question asked not by Ms.

Warden herself but something much more perilously spiritual that had momentarily occupied her body.

He could only muse on these conflicting thoughts for so long, before he begrudgingly picked up his cell phone. He first entered – *Jeff Gammon sexual abuse claims* – and then several variations of the same, all which brought up no more recent results than the few articles that were published back in 2018. "Allegations only", he whispered to himself. He could take just a modicum of relief from this, before managing to drink the first glass of water he had had that day. After he gulped it down, as if he was drinking it more for courage than hydration, he entered – *Randy Scanlon release* – and several variations on that. There was not much more information about it, but based on the most recent articles, he would be out soon. The prison was noted in the articles, but not a specific release date, which was likely intentional. Who knew what the family of Leslie Scanlon knew or how they felt about this? He knew from past articles that she had an older brother out of state. Her parents may have been too old to do much. She had no children, but at 36 the possibility was still there for her. The more Brian read about her, the more he sensed that there were few if any who could really speak for her. Who knew how committed any friends she had were to this, and had they even bothered writing letters of protest about her ex-husband's premature release. *18 months*, Brian mused with indignance. *18 months?!*

This question was the only thing that could momentarily put aside the seeming uselessness of his own life. And then it dawned on him…

He came upon the Department of Corrections website and, after entering in so much as Scanlon's name and age, he was able to obtain an exact date for his release from Branding Correctional Facility, which happened to be just an hour north of Crawberry, where he grew up: Tuesday, August 7th. *In two days.* He now knew when – as well as where.

He also knew that he'd be sick on Tuesday, as well. It was all quite clear to him now, as he looked at the screen, and mumbled – "My story is not yet written."

Seventeen

On the train heading upstate, he decided to call his sister Kim, as it'd been a while:

"Wow, I didn't expect this," Kim said, with genuine surprise in her voice.

"Didn't expect what?" Brian asked.

"Well,…frankly, you calling," she weakly laughed.

Brian could not take offense at this, as it *was* unusual for him to call, especially outside of the holiday season. They had not spoken since he had called in December telling her he wouldn't be able to come out for Christmas – the second consecutive one he would miss. Since Kim had the kids, and their father was alone but still able to get around, the last few years Christmas had been at Kim's house in Connecticut. There was nothing particularly warm about the event, as Brian looked back. It was just a rote gathering because they were related by blood. He never gave it much thought before but realized its superficiality all the more when he had changed his way of living. But, of course, it was also difficult to see his sister and father for the very reason that they reminded him of his old self. In truth, he only seemed to ever go out for the holidays out of habit – *that's what people do*, he used to think. *Even if they aren't particularly enamored by the company.*

"Yeah, a call in the summer. Look at that," he attempted to match her weak laughter, but it was futile.

"Are you okay?" she asked.

He couldn't think of a time that his sister asked this, except in relation to how things were in the city. She had always asked questions that were generalizations more than what was specific to him. "Uh, yeah. Why?"

"No, just… I didn't expect to hear from you. It's good to hear your voice."

He took this in, additionally not recalling a time when she had expressed particular joy from his call. She often seemed preoccupied and scattered in her attempts at conversation, with her family being the obvious excuse. Yet now it almost seemed as if she lived alone by how she behaved towards him.

"Yeah, it's…it's good to hear yours. How's the…how's the family?" he managed.

"Oh, they're good, thanks. Chuck's working a lot these days. He got promoted, so his reward is that he gets pretty much the same pay but more hours."

"Oh, jeez."

"Yep."

"Well,…congrats on his promotion anyway. I'm…I'm sure it means *some*thing."

"Eh, well. It's just been a coupla' months, so we'll see."

"The kids?" he asked, almost too quickly.

"Yeah, they're keeping us on our toes. Jillian got on the Honor Roll this year."

"Oh. Wow, nice," he forced enthusiasm.

"Yep. And Zack's playing, like, three different sports. We can't even keep up."

"Yeah?"

"Yep. He's like you when you were a kid."

He paused at this. "Really."

"Soccer, Baseball and Basketball. And he's an All-Star in everything. Just like you."

"Oh, well, that… I was an all-star just in baseball, I think. So Zack's got me beat pretty good."

"You weren't an all-star in basketball?"

"Uh, no."

"Not in soccer, either?"

"Uh,…no."

"I thought you were."

"No. Just played 'em."

"Hm," she mused on this, as Brian waited awk-wardly…

"Well, that's nice. That's…wow. Wonderful, Kim."

"Yep. So…we're all good."

"And you?"

Kim took a beat, as if not expecting this. "Good, good, thanks. Back to working full-time now that the kids are older."

"Oh, good. I mean, I assume it's good, right?"

"Yeah, well, that's the thing. It's real estate, so the market fluctuates and sometimes, for all the hours you put in, you still don't get the sales, but…such are the times we live in, right?"

"Yeah, I guess."

"Yep."

At this point, Brian felt it wise to end the call, as he wanted to take in the vast green landscapes he was passing, as he suspected it would be the last time he would see them in this way. The silence between he and Kim was now becoming apparent, before the train tooted…

"Oh, what's…? Are you on a train?"

"Uh, yeah, actually."

"Where're you going?"

He paused, realizing how absurd it would seem. "Gonna' visit dad."

"Really?" Kim again could not help but be surprised. "Does he know?"

"Yeah, of course he knows. I told him I was gonna' visit for a day. I didn't see him for his birthday, so…I figured now's as good a time as any."

"His birthday was in May," she said, amused.

He paused at this, "Yeah, I know, Kim. I couldn't… I was busy with things, and… Well, he's not big on birthdays anyway, so it's not like it matters."

"So why does it all of a sudden matter *now*?" Kim asked, more amused than pointed.

"What?"

"No, I'm not questioning why you're… I know he doesn't care about his birthday. Actually, he hates it. So why is this the reason to go out and see him?"

Brian now felt as if he had said too much. He should've just said he was going to see his father because he was passing through. That would've been more accurate. He *was* passing through, but he didn't want to reveal what he was passing through *to*. "I dunno'. I just wanted to see 'im. I have time off this week, so I figured…why not."

"Okay, well, good. It'll be good for him to see you."

"Has he been okay?"

"Yeah. You know him. We talked last month. You can never read him. He's to himself. I guess it was okay when he was married to Ellen, but now that he's alone in the house, it's a little odd. I mean, he's only 68, but you wonder."

"Wonder what?"

"He's getting older, Brian. And he's by himself. Something could happen, and… Well, listen, he's okay. He came for Christmas and he seemed fine. He'll be the same until…he's not here anymore. What can you say?"

Brian absorbed this. It was obvious that Kim having a family of her own gave her some perspective in dealing with their father now. They were likely no closer than he and Brian, but she was at least more in his life than Brian was and had tried to be the strand that provided any connection the family had. She could look at their father and see how her kids would one day be looking at Chuck – or her. What if they too were alone? What if they one day lived only to be a concern to their offspring?

Brian was alone now, and hadn't managed a wife or children, and yet it would be fine for him if he had managed anything else. The final destination of this trip, he concluded, was the one thing he could leave behind. The end of his story.

"Well, it'll be good to see him," he managed, as he observed the white colonial-style houses he had long recognized zipping by.

"Hey, how's your… You're still at the food place? Food-with…?"

"Food-*on*-Feet, yeah."

"How're things there?"

"It's…yeah, it's good. Getting people fed. That's…what we do."

"That's great, Brian," she said with obvious sincerity. "I know with all these cutbacks, it must be tough for a non-profit like that, right?"

"Yeah, but…you know, we do what we can with what we're given." He could not help but sound disappointed, for he could now not speak of his job without thinking of all the depressing aspects of it.

There was another odd silence between them. Then "You know, I think mom woulda' been proud of you."

Brian paused. "Why do you say that?"

"Well, you know, she did outreach stuff. She taught those poor kids on the weekends. That meant a lot to her. Probably more than anything. I just think she'd appreciate what you're doing there."

"Huh," Brian managed, at a loss of what else to say to this.

"I thought maybe that was why."

"Why what?"

"Well, you know, why you decided to change jobs. And the suicide hotline, and all. I thought maybe that could've had something to do with it."

It wasn't the reason, but he didn't want to take credit away from his dead mother. "Uh,…maybe. I didn't really… Yeah."

"Brian?" she asked, softly.

"Yeah?"

"Are you sure you're okay?"

It took him a moment to process Kim's question, and how it felt so foreign for her to ask in such a way. It was then that he felt the sudden urge to be honest in a way he had never been with his sister. He was on the verge of two paths, one of which would tell Kim everything because of a desperate need to reveal the why of this trip – and the other, which he opted for: "I'm good, Kim. Why do you keep asking that?" he weakly snickered.

She paused. "Nothing. Just…" The door slammed in the distance. "Sorry, hold on, Brian. Chuck, is that…?! Oh, it's… Hold on, Brian. Zack, cleats off, okay? Zack, did you hear me?! Off with those! We just had the floors redone!" she exclaimed in a tone of unequivocal motherliness.

Brian's stop was approaching, and it was just as well. And Kim would likely look at her son's boisterous entrance as a good excuse to wrap things up anyway.

"Brian?"

"Yeah, I'm here. Look, my – "

"You wana' say hi to your nephew?" she asked.

Brian paused. "I…I would, Kim, but my stop's almost here and I have to – " the train tooted. "I have to get my stuff together. I'll…I'll call later, okay?"

"Okay," her tone resonating disappointment. For some reason, it appeared now more than ever she wanted her kids to know their uncle was in their lives, but he still felt removed and, in that moment, very much wanted to be. She continued, "Listen, have a nice visit with dad. I'm sure he'll… I mean, he is who he is, but I'm sure it'll be a nice diversion for him."

"Yeah. Look, give my best to Zack…and Jillian and hi to Chuck, okay?" he rushed.

"Brian?"

He reluctantly paused. "Yeah?"

"Don't miss Christmas this year, okay?" The brakes began to squeal, as if to punctuate her request.

He couldn't bring himself to agree. "I'm…I'm losing you, Kim. Take care…" before he hung up, using the cacophonic sounds of the train to justify the abrupt disconnection. He sat there a moment, as the train eased to a stop. Again, he couldn't help but notice just how pleased she was to hear from him, as well as how concerned. He began to suspect that it wasn't just the many months that had passed. They had gone considerable stretches without talking over the years, and both seemed fine with it. It was never out of anger, just apathy combined with the fact that they were very dissimilar individuals. But this was different. *Was she picking up on something?*, he thought.

"Crawberry!" exclaimed a passing conductor. Brian looked out the window a moment, recalling how different he was the last time he pulled into this station.

He stood on the platform of Crawberry Station, with the midday sun in his eyes. He squinted to see business cards of a sole local cab company adorning a bulletin board near the benches, but decided he would walk to his father's. There was something about where he was at mentally now that made him not want to expedite things too much. A cab would get him to his father's in about 5 minutes, but to walk the 15 blocks to the house would have greater resonance. Before he started, he stood just outside the skeletal, unmanned train depot and observed how few businesses were nearby anymore. There was once a small general store called Sticky's that became a car wash that now was a hollowed-out structure of past establishments. There was a car repair shop that had also come and gone and was now a tacky Dollar store. There was a cellular phone shop and a pizza shop side-by-side. The latter had been a pizza place throughout Brian's existence, though the ownership continually changed, as the pizza got progressively worse. It had been about 4 years since Brian had been back to the house, as he'd mainly seen his father at Kim's for Christmas and, occasionally, Thanksgiving. Four years may not have been exceptionally long, but it amazed Brian how different it all seemed. He almost could not believe that this was a town that he came from. In the same moment, he began to recall what brought him to the city. He tried to remember his aspirations. *Did I really come all the way there to work as a security guard?*

As he walked, he began to remember. He had graduated from the local community college with degrees in hospitality and public relations. He couldn't fathom now why he had chosen those two, as they were of almost no use to his future pursuits. However, the catalyst for him moving to the city was that he had been offered a job at a hotel in midtown Manhattan, recommended by a former classmate of his, Tony, whom he had since lost touch with. Brian worked at the hotel as a front desk clerk for about a year before discovering through another colleague that he could make more money as a security guard for corporate buildings. And there he stayed, in the same position but at various interchangeable buildings in mid-and-lower Manhattan for almost 15 progressively numbing years. Up until a few weeks ago, he had considered himself to be at the most productive stage of his life and career. He really did believe he was helping and considered himself to be a sponge willing to absorb anything that would make him a better human being. But even that was a great distance away from where he was now.

He stood on the corner of Essex and Kendall, now just about 8 blocks from his destination, as he observed the house of David O'Lagley. He didn't know if his family still lived there, though it looked the same. In an instant, he felt a deep sadness and that sick feeling in his stomach that had now become too common for him. He hardly knew David in middle school but at some point in high school David would sometimes become the object of Brian and Kirk's taunts. Particularly one time when they were walking home from school. Brian and Kirk were a tandem for much of Brian's sophomore year. David walked ahead of them, always in a strange bopping manner that was rife for mocking. Brian and Kirk would often just comment to each other: "That kid walks like someone's constantly goosin' him, right?" Brian would ask, to which Kirk would say, "More like he's gettin' a rectal exam and he's enjoying it."

But one day, something made Kirk become more vocal, which would only inspire Brian. As they walked home, Kirk shouted "Hey, do you walk to some sorta' music in your head, Davey?!" Brian laughed, as they sped up behind David, as he neared his house. Then Brian would start singing his own rendition of the Oompa Loompa song from *Willie Wonka and the Chocolate Factory*, which had a distinct and somewhat abrasive rhythm to it:

"Oompa Loompa, doobadeedoo –
I bop when I walk, with my shorts full of poo."

They sang this same made-up second line to the rhythm of David's walk louder and more obnoxiously, which soon forced David to speed up, as Brian and Kirk picked up speed themselves. As their singing got louder and their tempo increased, David eventually got to the steps of his house, but in his eagerness to evade them he tripped and banged his front teeth on the top step. This brought about uproarious laughter from both Brian and Kirk, as David covered his mouth before scampering into his house.

A couple of days later, Brian saw David in the cafeteria and noticed that he was eating his food in a strange manner. It turned out he was eating in such a way because he lost his tooth and didn't want to cut his gums while eating. Kirk still made fun of him from afar, but Brian felt their brief foray into being bullies had run its course. He never said anything to Kirk, except to stop acknowledging when he would make fun of someone. By the end of their sophomore year, Kirk moved out of state with his family. Brian never had to confront him about his behavior, which now bothered him. *Was it only because he moved that I didn't hang out with him into my junior year?* he asked himself. *He was an asshole, and I was his friend. He probably became someone like Randy Scanlon, I bet. A fucking brute.*

He was still at the same corner looking at the door to David O'Lagley's house, and wondered where he was. What kind of life was he living? Were his parents alive? But he couldn't dwell. He wanted to take his time on this walk, but this wasn't productive.

Eighteen

His father opened the door.

"Oh, hey," he said mildly. "I forgot when ya' said."

"Um,…today," Brian replied, awkwardly.

"I thought it was… Well, hey, you're here. How was the traffic?"

"I didn't drive," as Brian walked in. His father sauntered back into the living room, as if his day would not change, regardless of this visit.

"You didn't drive?" as he sat back in his desk chair, before his laptop computer.

"No, I don't have a car. I haven't had one since I've lived in the city."

"Oh. Makes sense, I guess. Enough congestion there anyway, right?"

Brian paused, taken aback by the casualness of his father and how his presence barely seemed to resonate with him. "Yeah, there's…there's a lot of people in the city. How've you been?"

His father looked at the screen, "Not bad. Gettin' some rest." His father then turned his full focus to an article online, as a silence sat between them.

Brian observed him, but was loath to ask the source of his transfixion. It wasn't a real surprise that his father wouldn't have much to say – he never did. But now that he was there, Brian somehow hoped he'd get something more from him this trip, as he watched him from behind. "Is…is it okay if I use the bathroom?"

"You don't have to ask. You grew up here, for Godsakes," which seemed to be the first acknowledgement that Brian was, at the very least, a former resident. Brian put his backpack on the couch, then walked to the bathroom adjacent to the kitchen. He threw some water in his face, then looked in the mirror as drops cascaded from his chin. In the moment, it felt like this would be the last time he would see himself, or care to. Through his reflection, he saw his childhood. He remembered when this very bathroom had the tackiest violet wallpaper. It changed to the tan color it was now by the time he was in junior high. He remembered when he would read *Rolling Stone* and *Sports Illustrated* magazines on the toilet until his legs fell asleep, which used to prompt door knocks from Kim or his mother when his father was occupying the one upstairs. He wished he had more fond memories of this bathroom – or the house surrounding it – but it was little more to him than a storage area for his developing years; no more memorable than a stable might be to a horse. It was just as well. He didn't plan to return.

He came out to see his father still immersed at his computer desk. "Whatcha' readin'?" Brian asked, without interest.

"Oh, just this chat thingy I belong to."

"A chat room?"

"Yeah, I guess. Just having an interesting conversation."

"What kind of chat room?"

"It's mainly topical. Politics. People sharing opinions. It's interesting."

"Is it all the same opinion?" Brian asked.

"Whata' y'mean?" his father followed, without turning to him.

"I mean, are there different points of view or all the same?"

"Sometimes it's about different points of view of the same view. It's interesting."

Brian walked closer to his father and quickly caught a response from someone: *They don't have a clue. If they knew what was right for this country, they wouldn't let every Tom, Dick and Harry in to take our jobs!*

Right then and there, he knew what this was and had little interest in discussing it with his father. He had been a mild conservative for much of Brian's life, but Brian never really gauged a more specific political view of him since it never interested him, nor did it interest his mother or Kim. But it seemed, quite possibly, that the events of the last few years combined with the dormancy of retirement, had started to send him down a cyber rabbit hole. *Could this have even contributed to his divorce?* he wondered.

It didn't really matter. His father's political views or even Brian's relationship with his father wasn't really the reason he was there.

"I'm gonna' put my stuff in my room, if that's cool."

His father finally turned to face him, and appeared stunned that he only had a small backpack.

"That's all you got?"

Brian paused. "Yeah. I'm not staying long."

"How long ya' stayin'?"

All of sudden, Brian felt obligated to be delicate in cryptically explaining the brevity of his trip. He naively thought his father would likely be so aloof, that he could stay the night and leave in the morning without so much as a reason. Now it appeared one was needed.

"I'm only...um...I can only stay one night, dad. I have somewhere to be."

"Where's 'at?"

"Um...I have to see...an old friend, further upstate."

"Where?"

He swallowed, "Branding."

"What the heck's up there?"

"Well, this…this old friend of mine. He's…he's going through… He asked my help for something. I had a few days off from work, so I thought I'd see you n'then see him."

"Who do you know up there? Someone from school?"

Brian was continually surprised by his father's interest. "No. He's… A more recent person. I know him from the city. From…from Queens, actually. He…moved, and he's… It's kinda' personal, dad. If you don't mind."

His father sat with this, as if he had never absorbed anything Brian had said to him before so thoroughly. "Alright," he muttered, then turned back to his computer. Brian watched him scroll through what looked like a tome of cyber dialogue, before heading upstairs.

It had only been four years, but everything seemed so small to him, and yet it was all very much frozen in time. The stairs still creaked the same with every step. The walls remained the same. The pictures. The furniture. There was no trace of another's touch – it was as if his second marriage was so short, there was barely time for Ellen to impose any stylistic choices. He barely thought of where she was now. The marriage's dissolution was astonishing in its uneventfulness. No one seemed to care. But he could still sense his mother, and that was at once the most distinctive and the saddest thing about his return home. She had designed the interior of this house, and barely a hair had changed, except for the computer and computer desk and possibly some linens, but even that was doubtful.

He threw his backpack on his bed, looked out the window at the quiet street, but barely took time to absorb the bland view, which had no distinction among any middle-class neighborhood in rural upstate New York.   He went to the stairs and could hear the tapping of the keyboard keys from below, before he was assured that now was as good a time as any. He went into his father's room, walking at the volume and pace of a seasoned cat burglar, before seeing the closet. He knew it was there. As he slid open the door, he looked at the top shelf where his father always kept his shoebox. As he touched it, he could feel the dust – the box had likely never been touched since he purchased the gun, back when Brian's mother was alive, in response to burglaries that had been reported in the area at the time. He slowly removed the box and placed it on the floor, so delicately as if in fear that somehow it could detonate like a grenade. He pulled away the layers of old musty shoe rags, and there it was. It was the first time Brian had seen the gun since his father brought it home and, like just about everything else in the house, it had been unchanged. The box even contained the receipt from where he purchased it, as if his father thought he could someday return it, even decades later. The typed receipt noted it as a Taurus .38 Special Snub Nose.

Prior to leaving his apartment, he looked up videos on how to check for bullets and how to load them, should the gun be empty. He had never handled a gun before. He knew movies would not be an accurate tutorial, but in the internet era, there indeed were many videos that went over this. However, he wasn't sure of the gun type in his initial research, and so now that he knew, he would need to revisit – but certainly not while he was at the house. For now, he would take the gun and a few bullets which were loose within the shoebox. Before he resumed preparing it for transport, he tiptoed back to the bedroom doorway to make sure that the coast was clear, then quickly returned, wrapped the gun and bullets in some of the rags before slipping them into his backpack, which contained all of one pair of underwear and socks. He placed the shoebox back in the closet, then went to his old room. Suddenly, he heard his father approach the foot of the stairs…

"Brian?!"

Brian jumped off the bed on which he'd just sat down. "Uh, ye… yeah, dad?!"

"You hungry?"

They sat across from each other at the Jolly Diner, which could not have been more in opposition to its name. The diner had been in Crawberry for the whole of Brian's life and, at this point, it was all but a shell of its former, if modest, glory. The waitress lugubriously took their order, as if she was in mourning, then left. Brian wasn't really hungry, but he had to do something with his father during the short time he was there.

"Grilled cheese? That's it?" his father asked.

"Yeah."

"Why not get meat loaf or a sirloin steak or somethin'?"

"I'm really not that hungry, dad. Anyway, I don't really eat meat anymore."

"What, you're a vegetarian now?"

"Uh, I have fish on occasion, but I haven't eaten meat for a while."

"Any particular reason?"

"Uh, just…because it felt right."

"What's wrong about having meat loaf? You can have it."

"Well, I know I *can* have it, but I choose not to."

"Hm, okay," his father nodded, then moved his folded napkin slightly to the left for no particular reason, then looked out the window.

Brian tried to use this opportunity to savor whatever he could of his father's presence, for he was now certain that he would not see him again in this way. But he struggled to seek topics for discussion with him. He wasn't even sure if his father remembered what he was doing for a living, and at this point he had little desire to remind him. For all the changes in

Brian's life, it didn't appear to register with his father – but it wasn't necessarily surprising.

"So Kim sounds good," Brian forced a grin, as he sipped his water.

"You talked to 'er?"

"Yeah. I called her on the train. They all seem to be doing well."

"Yeah, seems so."

"How was Christmas there?"

"Christmas?"

"Yeah, you were there, right?"

"Have we not spoken since then?"

Brian paused. "We spoke briefly on the phone that day."

"Jeez, I don't even remember. I guess it was all right. That's right, you weren't there, were ya'."

Brian paused again. "No. I called but, no, I wasn't there."

"What happened, work?"

"Well, on Christmas I was volunteering."

"Oh, yeah. The year before, too, right?"

"Uh, yeah."

"What, a homeless shelter?"

"Soup kitchen."

"Aren't they more-or-less the same thing?"

"No, dad. Soup kitchens serve food to homeless, but they don't house them. It's two different things."

"Oh, I see."

"Mhm," as Brian moved his own napkin, for no particular reason.

"Everything else okay?"

Brian was taken aback by the inquiry; trying to decipher if these were the usual surface questions or a continuation of Kim's concern. "Uh, it's…yeah, I guess."

"You're at that… What is it? The Food-with-Feet…?"

"Food-*on*-Feet, yeah."

"Right. I guess that's a lota' work, huh?"

"It…it is what it is. It has its challenges."

"You go out and see folks who wana' have their meals delivered?"

"Yeah, exactly," Brian was momentarily impressed at his father's knowledge of this, or at least the fact that what little he mentioned to him about it some time ago still resonated, when it more often appeared that he was in his own world.

His father nodded, almost approvingly, then turned back to the window and the passing cars. "Yeah, I guess I may be gettin' them one day. They have branches out here?"

Brian paused at this, stunned that his father had such a lucid plan for a time when he might not be competent enough to fend for himself. "Well, there's probably similar organizations that you can look into. Why do you say you'll be getting them?"

"Well, unless you up'n die of a heart attack some-day soon, it's likely that you'll live to have impairments of one kind or another. And when you're by yourself,..." He trailed off. By *you*, of course, he meant himself and people of his generation. He wasn't sentimental in the slightest, but more observational, and so he could talk about his eventual demise without sadness, as if he was referencing someone else. It was much more difficult for Brian to have his father theorize that he would die alone. He would likely never remarry. He would likely never have much of a desire to begin again with another woman. He would be fine to do the same thing every day and just appreciate the fact that he didn't have to go to a job that he hated. That was as much gold as he could siphon for his golden years.

Brian felt handcuffed as to how to proceed. He could offer to help him when that time came, but since he was certain that he wouldn't be around to do so, it felt wrong to lead him on. He could only take comfort in the fact that his father wasn't the type to rely on anyone. He was prideful, at least that way. Anyway, Kim would be able to help. If his father could just manage another few years on his own, Kim's kids would be old enough and she could then be more productive in assisting him; dealing with Medicare, and the awful healthcare bureaucracy that Brian was now familiar with. And then, just as quickly, he felt bad to have her in that position. She was the younger sibling, after all. The responsibility chain should ideally fall to the eldest when it came to their parents' care. He could only take solace in the fact that he wasn't an only child. There would be *someone*, provided nothing happened to Kim. And then he recalled their conversation, and how concerned she seemed and unusually interested in his work, and even complimentary of his career change. Did it all ultimately stem from having been so disappointed in him for not aspiring to more earlier?

Then, as if a sudden gastric slippage, "How 'bout those Mets?" his father asked, with a tepid grin.

Brian swallowed his water down the wrong pipe, at what this question summoned. Not only did he still have no idea how the Mets were doing but, more overwhelmingly, it made him recall his utterly disastrous meeting with Chad. He even forgot that his father was a Mets fan and, of course, now wished he wasn't.

After several coughs, "Yeah, I heard they're…doing okay."

"Division leaders," his father said with a sudden pride.

"Oh, yeah?"

"What, you don't know?"

"To be honest, dad, I stopped following."

"Baseball?"

"All of it."

"No sports? Really?"

"Yeah."

"My God, you used to live'n breathe it."

He looked out the window, as his father did, then looked back at his father's profile – and recalled his parents cheering him from the bleachers during his Little League games. Back then, his father even assumed Brian would pursue sports more seriously and even get a scholarship to a major college. But none of that happened, nor did Brian have those aspirations. Was his father disappointed in him? He would never know unless he asked, and it was foolish to. However, it did seem as if his father was taken aback that he no longer followed sports, especially the Mets. It was now just one less thing for them to talk about, as their food arrived.

His father stuck his fork in his chicken pot pie, then let the steam exit out of the opening in the crust. "So what do you do?"

Brian picked up his uninspired grilled cheese, which he would soon discover had the flavor of a toasted sponge. "Whata' you mean?"

"Just…for fun. To pass the time."

Brian paused again. Every such question now was not unlike his lunch with Vanessa. He needed to think before answering, because the why of things was too complicated. "Well, I've tried to donate my time to things, when I can."

"Like what?"

"Charity events. That kinda' thing. I've told you this before. I volunteer at a suicide hotline."

"My God, you pass the time at a suicide hotline?" his father couldn't help but smile as he said it.

"No, I just… It's just something I do."

"Okay. Well,…that's good, Brian. I didn't mean to make light. That's important." His father meant it, as much as he could.

Brian paused. "Thanks," he replied, without much conviction, then took another spongey bite, while attempting to lighten the tone: "I read a lot."

"Yeah? Stephen King's gotta' new one out, I heard. You read that one?"

"Uh, no, I don't read that kinda'… More like spiritual-based stuff. New age," then he swallowed, "Self-help."

"Self-help."

"Yeah."

"You need helping?" his father asked, with an unusual smile.

Brian couldn't appreciate it as a jest, nor could he find an easy answer in any other way. "Improving, I guess. I've tried to…better myself. It takes effort. It takes focus. And…I guess I've never really had it. So…I've tried."

"You still believe in God?" his father asked, just as he gulped the first piece of his pie.

"What?" Brian asked, stunned.

His father swallowed, "You believe in God, still?"

Brian was raised to automatically assume His existence. And over the course of the last nearly two years, he was more committed to believing – but now everything for him was in question.   He didn't want to complicate things by saying anything other than "Yes," before his father nodded, as if assured that Brian hadn't gone completely off the rails.

On the drive back, his father asked, "Wana' grab a drink?"

Brian had never had a drink with his father, and didn't even drink anymore. The question had an air of loneliness to it, as if his father was seizing every opportunity to be what he rarely ever was, particularly at this stage of his life – social.

"Uh, sure. I don't drink anymore, but…"

"You don't drink either?"

Brian paused at his further surprise. "No."

"Jeez, no sports, no alcohol?" his father shook his head.

"I mean, I can have a Coke or something. It's not like I have to drink booze, right?"

His father paused, as he pulled into the only local bar, Granley's Pub, as he nodded with some disappointment, "True."

They sat at the bar, with a few scattered patrons in booths having various pub grub; most notably burgers, fish and chips… After his father ordered a Guinness, Brian's sudden guilt prompted him to order the same, as if his father would seem less alone by the gesture:

"There ya' go," his father noted, modestly pleased. "You know it has alcohol, now."

Brian tepidly smiled, "Yeah, I know."

His father looked around, as if a tourist taking in the sites.

"You come here a lot?" Brian asked.

"Me? No. Jeez, I haven't been here in… God, I don't know when. You?"

"Me? Well, I don't live here, dad."

"I know that. I mean, were you ever here?"

"Uh, yeah, I came a few times when I was in college, I think. Seems the same."

"We never came together?" his father asked.

Brian thought, "No, I don't think so."

"Even for dinner? With your mom'n Kim?"

Brian thought again. "No, I don't recall."

His father seemed struck by this, as he looked around. "Well, it's a Goddamn dive anyway. I mean, the Shepherd's pie ain't bad, but…" as his recollections faded in their importance.

The bartender brought their drinks and, to Brian's surprise, his father gestured that this would be the first round of an ongoing tab. His father took a sip, savored it for a moment. Brian was not particularly desiring of imbibing, but indulged him with his own. "Definitely came here with your mom," his father mumbled.

"Yeah?"

"Before we got married, then for a few times after. She liked the fish'n chips."

"Huh," Brian thought, then recalled, "Yeah, I remember she liked those."

"She did."

"I think she ordered them when we went to Disney World or some place like that."

"They had fish'n chips at Disney?" his father asked, skeptically.

"It mighta' not been there. Some place like it. Maybe Epcot."

"Nah, wouldn'ta' been there. Fish'n chips at Epcot Center?"

"I dunno'. Maybe I just dreamed it," Brian finally managed, with a sudden appearance of sarcasm.

His father looked at him, "Dreamed it? You can't think of better dreams than your mother ordering fish'n chips at an amusement park?"

"I'm joking, dad," Brian needed to note.

His father didn't know how to take his jest, or his subtle defensiveness. He turned back to his beer. "Anyway, we ate here. It was a nice memory."

Brian felt bad in getting short with his father. He never really had before, since they never had long enough exchanges to warrant it. Or at least it felt that way. But he was anxious in that this was likely to be the last time he would see his father as mutual citizens of the free world. He didn't know what he wanted from him, and wondered if he really wanted anything from him aside from his gun. But now he was trans-fixed by his father's mention of his mother, especially in such a pleasant, nostalgic way. It just wasn't some-thing he ever did – at least Brian never witnessed it himself. Perhaps his father may've said something to Kim, but he doubted it. His father was old school enough wherein if any deep emotions were to come out, it would be to a man before a woman – particu-larly his elder son, as opposed to his younger daughter. But it was only the beginning.

"Shouldn'ta' got remarried," he followed, after an-other retrospective sip.

Brian paused. "Why did you?"

"Eh, Ellen was nice enough. But we weren't in love. Just lonely. But I wasn't very nice to her once we started living together. It was like…we went on some dates, spent time together. Seemed to get along well enough. Then she moved in, and…and I think I picked up with her where I left off with your mother."

Brian was now forgetting where he was. For all he knew, his father and he were in a confessional booth together, and he was now Father Devon, with all the sounds of the outside world hushed to a sudden si-lence. "Whata' you mean?" he asked.

His father stared at his reflection in the mirror be-hind the bar. "I sorta' got numb in the last years of our marriage. I hated by job, I was exhausted. She didn't much care for her job, but it was a diversion she needed.   The house was just a place where the bed'n the couch were," he sipped. "She wasn't happy."

There was something about his last statement which resonated in an unusual way with Brian.   He was all but certain that those three words were not a throwaway observation. Several factors told him this. One, his training and experience at the suicide hotline helped him with his listening skills. It was the first time he forced himself to be a listener more than an orator. He had no choice there but to be a supportive presence, and to catch phrases that might not reveal much on the surface but, ultimately, were intended to generate a question – and from the listener's question would often come a revelation, of sorts. In that moment, he thought of Robert and what had happened to him after their enlightening discussion about the *I Ching. Why did he never call back?* And just as quickly, it left his mind and was replaced by the man in front of him. There needn't be any such ambiguity here, because they were in this pub together, and he could ask questions, if he felt so compelled. He could be brutally honest, if he needed to be. What on this green earth did he have to lose anyway? This was his father. He knew this man. He was half the reason why Brian existed. He knew his flaws. He knew all the things about him that he grew to detest about himself. He knew that for his father to reveal his mother's unhappiness was to put at least a considerable amount of blame on himself. He may've thought this for a while now. He may've said this to someone else, but Brian strongly doubted it. What it seemed was that his father knew he was getting older. He would be 70 soon. He sensed his mortality. He had no particular legacy to leave behind. The company in which he gave over 30 years of his life likely had no nostalgia for his contributions, and probably little memory. He was a lonely man living in the same old house. He could only hope that his death would come suddenly, on his couch, before some mindless television news show – as opposed to living beyond his lucid years, to be adorned with IV bags and machinery.

When all was said and done, the least he could be was honest.

"She was seein' someone, y'know," he mumbled.

It was as if Brian knew this was coming, and yet he still couldn't help but be stunned. "You mean, while you were…?"

"Yep," his father chirped, still staring at his reflection in the mirror.

Brian took a moment, both for himself and in respect for his father's emotions. "When was this?"

"Last coupla' years, before she died. Mainly on Saturdays."

This was worse, Brian felt. Because… *No*, he thought.

"You know she said she was teaching those kids on Saturdays?'

Brian swallowed, and barely managed… "She never did?"

"She did,…for a little while. Then the program got cancelled. Budget issues. They couldn't keep it going, even though she was volunteering."

"I don't understand."

His father sipped, took a breath. He was about to speak before the bartender walked by, then when he walked to the other end, he resumed: "There was another volunteer she met. He was also married. They started grabbing a bite after classes, before she'd come home. They hadn't done anything at that point, but there was… There was somethin' there. Then when they found out the program got cancelled, I guess, they thought they could still use it as an excuse to see each other. So they did."

Brian could barely speak. Only the ambient clinking of glasses could be heard now. Then, "For…for how long?"

"About a year or so. Until she was diagnosed."

He swallowed again, not wanting to ask, but having little choice now. "So…most of the time she was away on Saturdays, she was…?"

His father nodded, before finally turning to Brian. Brian had never seen his father's face so focused and apologetic before. But he did nothing more beyond that. No words or tears. He then turned back to the mirror, sipped his Guinness.

After another long silence, "When did she tell you?", Brian asked.

"She didn't."

Brian was stunned, yet again. "Then…?"

"Was going through her stuff after she passed. Came across her diary."

"She kept a diary?"

"Yep. Diary, journal, whatever. Anyway, flipped through it. I'd never read her entries before, but…there it was."

After another long silence. "Does Kim know?"

His father shook his head. "She doesn't need to," then sipped again.

Brian sat with this for a moment. "Why are you telling *me*?"

His father continued looking at the mirror, clutching his glass. "Didn't expect to."

This was confounding for Brian. Why did his father feel compelled? It further put into question why all of this was occurring now. He wasn't on his death bed. Why did he have the need to reveal this, especially when he certainly couldn't be classified as remotely inebriated after all of six sips of Guinness. Further, why was Kim acting so concerned? Why was his normally distant family all of sudden so transparent in their feelings? Was it partly as a result of his absence from recent holiday gatherings? And, finally, what was he to do with this knowledge about his mother? After feeling initially ignored by her for the time she gave to volunteering, he grew to appreciate what she did – even if it could be partially excused as an escape from her marriage, which his father readily admitted had devolved into catatonia. But to learn that only a portion of those Saturdays saw her actually giving her time to the less fortunate, and the majority were likely in some cheap motel room somewhere, was sickening to him. It was a betrayal. Not only as his mother but even more as an alleged altruist. All the things that Jeff Gammon had espoused – all the things that Brian strove for since shortly after the death of Leslie Scanlon, he had also wanted to attribute them to his mother. Someone who gave back before it was fashionable. Before people posted their graciousness online for all to envy.

She was just fucking around, he brooded.

They drove back to the house in silence, except for his father asking what train he wanted to catch.

Brian took a moment, his mind being elsewhere. "I was planning to catch the 9:20."

His father nodded, then "We'll have breakfast and I'll drop you off."

"Dad, that's alright."

"Whata' you mean?"

"You don't have to drop me."

"How'll ya' get there? You don't have a car."

"I'll walk."

"Walk?"

"It's just a few blocks. I'll be fine."

"Brian, I'm fine to take you. We'll eat, and I'll bring you over."

Brian couldn't keep arguing without it becoming potentially hurtful to him. He'd never thought much about being delicate with his father, but the revelations of the evening gave him a justifiable reason to be sensitive to his simple request. But it was a dreaded thought to have a symbolic last drive to the train with him. And who knows what else his father would reveal on the way there? The floodgates appeared to be open, and Brian was ill prepared. He had learned enough.

He asked his father about the whereabouts of his mother's diary, which was the only remaining curiosity he had on the subject. He had assumed his father couldn't bear to hold on to something that held such hurtful and salacious entries.

"It's in the basement," he managed, as they pulled into the driveway, before he pulled out the key. "Did you want it?"

Brian couldn't believe his ears. "What?"

"I didn't know if it was something you'd want."

"Why would I want *that*?"

"She's your mother."

That wasn't an attribute anymore, in Brian's eyes. And he was nauseous at the thought of having it. Knowing what he now knew, it would be like owning incestuous porn.

If nothing else, he knew his father wasn't making it up. It wasn't as if he brought it up to badmouth Brian's mother, for he took enough responsibility for her going astray. It just wouldn't make sense for him to create her infidelity – especially how he revealed it. Brian would take his father's word – and that would be enough.

That night, he lay in his childhood bed. Despite what he told his father, he already knew he was going to get the 6:20am train, which would have him in Branding by 7:30am. He would then get a car from a rental place he had already been in touch with, and be at the prison gate by roughly 8am. Scanlon's release on the Department of Corrections site was not specific in terms of the time of his release, but Brian knew that tomorrow was the day – and he would wait all day, if necessary.

Now not only was tomorrow's itinerary coursing through his brain, but also what came out during his evening with his father. It still pained him to hear what was revealed, but at the same time, it seemed to add fuel to his mission. There would be no doubt that, despite what he came from, despite what little he had achieved in his life, despite his cowardice, despite every adverse experience he was recalling in the moment, Randy Scanlon would not be free to one day impart the same fate on another woman.

He woke up at 5am, after possibly twenty minutes of sleep. He resorted to his cat burglar steps in order to avoid waking his father, whose unmistakable buzzsaw snoring reverberated from down the hall. He was already dressed and packed by 5:15am, and decided to walk to the basement. It was one of many things which had kept him up during the night – his mother's written documentation of a love affair with a fellow volunteer teacher. It took something of this enormity to even compete with his thoughts of the impending day. He tiptoed down the steps and stopped at every creak and squeal from the old wooden stairs, until he made it to the kitchen. From there, he laid his backpack on a chair by the kitchen table, then slowly walked down the even older and creakier basement steps. The dust and damp smell seemed to have no other recourse but to age and become only more pungent. His father's workbench remained, though it looked as if it had gone untouched since his mother's death. There were a few boxes of loose family photos and even trophies that Brian had amassed between junior high and high school, which he had no desire to look through.

Then he saw it – a box marked *Joan.*

It wasn't sealed, so he opened it up to see some of her favorite novels and art books, as well as a jar with her jewelry, which included a necklace that Brian had made for her in art class when he was around nine. He pulled it out delicately and held it up. The chain was made of silver and hooked onto it was a small piece of blown glass he remembered making himself, with a crudely etched *J* on it. Suddenly, he was overcome with emotion, but contained himself. He didn't want to wake his father and he didn't want his emotions to soften, on this day of all days.

He placed the necklace back in the jar, rummaged further, before seeing it – a 6 inch by 6 inch book with a crimson cover. He had never seen this before, but knew without question that this was the infamous diary. He didn't want to peruse any other pages but the ones that would most likely be relevant to what his dad had mentioned. All entries were dated. He came upon – *June 12th, 1998* – then read the following:

Wayne asked me if I was happy in my marriage. We've now had several weeks worth of lunches, and it's been obvious how we feel about each other. I feel bad, for the obvious reasons. But being married to Jim has become like being married to a mirage. Insubstantial.

Then Brian flipped ahead a couple of pages:

July 26th, 1998 –
It finally happened between Wayne and I. I don't know how I feel, exactly. We're attracted to each other and the love we shared was enjoyable – if completely foreign to me. Jim never kissed me like that, probably

ever. Still, I know it's wrong. Life feels so strange to me now.

Brian's emotions over the necklace were now quite distant, replaced by a building nausea that accumulated with every word. If he had possessed even an iota of disbelief regarding what his father claimed, these entries alone were enough to dispel it. He closed the box and kept the book. It was now 5:50. He tiptoed back up the steps until he was in the kitchen, then looked up the stairs to assure that his father was still asleep. He then placed the diary in his backpack, alongside his father's rag-wrapped .38 Special and bullets. He took a moment to look around the home that he was raised in, fearing a tear may come; a certain sweet memory; a holiday. Anything.

But there was nothing.

So he left.

The morning eyes of the sky were slowly opening, as Brian walked along the quiet roads en route to the train station. He stopped again at the corner of Essex and Kendall, looked at David O'Lagley's old house one last time. Again, he wondered if his family was still there. If David was alive. He could've asked his father, but he was fairly sure that he never knew them. As Brian remained still at the corner, and gazed at the house's front door, he issued a silent apology, for what it was worth, then turned to the road ahead. The silence surrounding him made it seem as if he was already in some sort of netherworld; a place he might likely end up after his life on this earth had concluded. And in momentarily believing it, he walked on, as his emotions regarding everything began to harden like clay. He wouldn't be fearful. He wouldn't idle. He knew what had to be done.

Eventually, the train arrived.

Nineteen

—

He sat in the predominately empty train car, thirty minutes into his trip. He gripped his mother's diary as he carefully eyed the passing domiciles, before the first body of water would appear: a lake, which he knew would suffice. He looked around the car to make sure no one was watching, before he pulled open the top portion of his seat window, and tossed the diary into the water, to be read by no one but the illiterate sea life. He quickly closed the window, then sat back down and took a deep breath, as if in relief that the first of his two primary goals of the day were met. He would look around again, seeing only the three scattered sleeping commuters, before he would take his bag to the restroom.

Now that he actually had his father's gun in his possession, he re-watched the video tutorial he had saved on his phone, as his heart began to race. He pointed the gun into the toilet, which felt like the safest place to aim it, as he opened the cylinder, per the red-bearded video instructor who looked as if he was born holding a firearm – adorned in a cigarette-burned Metallica t-shirt and jeans. Brian then carefully loaded each round into the five holes, before closing it. He felt the secure snap, which meant that the cylinder was locked.

Then he re-watched the *How-to-Shoot* episode of this bearded man's tutorial, which warned to avoid placing one's forefingers in the front of the cylinder, nearest to the gun's snub nose, as the heat that would generate after shooting would be fierce. *Boy, they don't tell you this in the movies*, Brian thought. Just as quickly, he couldn't help but note the absurdity: *What the hell does it matter if I burn my fingers after killing him?*

As he came out of the restroom, he was stunned to discover that there were now a few more people in the car, which made him feel as if someone knew his intent. He went back to his seat, now beginning to perspire, and clutched his backpack, which contained the newly-loaded revolver wrapped in his father's old shoe rags. He looked out the window at the houses zipping by, an occasional lake or river of varying size, a silo, a large empty patch of grass which was so green, it looked as if it had never been walked on. His discarding of his mother's innermost thoughts into the nameless lake was a distant memory now, replaced by his obsessive planning. He went over it in his head:

- *The gun's loaded.*
- *I just need to get a cab to the rental place. Then tell them I'm renting for the day. I don't have to worry about returning it because...*
- *Drive to the prison entrance. Wait.*

He discovered a photo image online of the prison entrance. It looked like any other prison he had seen in films and television. It was typically ominous, complete with circular barbed wire, a watch tower and what looked to be a sliding metal gate. He imagined he could park just outside without issue. He wasn't sure what else he should expect. *Other people? Law enforcement guarding the outside?* It was all the unknown. But it wasn't as if his plan was to run and flee. It was, undoubtedly, to shoot and then let the guards or whoever was in sight do what was required. If that meant kill Brian, so be it. If that meant giving him a chance to toss his gun away and be arrested, so be it. But Brian was determined that his ultimate objective would be achieved.

The train arrived at Branding Station.

He took a cab to the nearest car rental shop, his backpack held to his chest like a nervous freshman on his first day of high school. As he arrived at the shop, he was unsettled to discover that he was the only customer. It was early morning, and God knows how many people actually rented cars there. Branding wasn't known for much else but their prison and some factories which likely employed more people in neighboring towns than in Branding proper.

"Jus' for the day, y'said?" asked the burly man, who appeared to have just risen, without aid of a shower or comb.

"Ye…yes." Brian continuously looked at the door, somehow still thinking that someone had access to his brain and was hellbent on stopping him before it was too late.

After the charge was run through, the man slid Brian the keys gruffly across the counter. He went out with Brian, opened the driver's side door for him: "Take a look'n make sure whatever damage you see was already there."

Brian didn't grasp this, at first. "You… I'm sorry, you want me to look for damage?"

The man took this in, loath to reiterate. "Yeah. You don't wana' be blamed for a ding that's already there, right?"

Brian got it, but his nerves made it difficult for him to absorb even the most basic communication. He looked inside the car, and could not find a flaw, but wasn't looking carefully. "Okay, it's fine."

"Outside?" the man followed, gruffly.

"It's fine," Brian tersely replied.

"You didn't even…"

"Do you have what you need from me, sir?"

The man was now struck by Brian's sudden impatience. "You just have to sign this…"

Brian sharply took the pen from the man's clipboard, signed what looked like a form assuring he would be responsible for any new damage to the car… "There." Brian then shut the door, pulled out and sped off, before any hidden trepidation might surface.

He slowed down to avoid getting a ticket, as he navigated through the country roads, which had little distinction to them other than the trees on either side, though it was predominately a long, straight road to the prison.

He drove for about 20 minutes before he came upon it: the entrance to Branding Correctional Facility, just like in the online image he researched. Seeing the barbed wire in-person was jolting, because why it was there made its existence all the more real. Convicts had likely once escaped from there, or they had at least tried, at some point. Men who had by and large been convicted of unspeakable crimes, he thought. Why Randy Scanlon was even getting the opportunity to walk away from it after a year and a half was all the more absurd now that Brian was at the prison doorstep. He couldn't speak for anyone else that was there, as he didn't know them. Most were likely there justifiably, while a few may've been falsely accused. But there was no question why Randy Scanlon was there. None. Brian was an eyewitness, after all. He watched the entire event again, as he sat in the car across the silent road, approximately 30 yards away from the gate. He was standing beside Chad, and among others who had gradually amassed. They watched Leslie scream at Randy that he wasn't to come within 100 yards of her, and she wouldn't allow him in her apartment. He remembered even then thinking how ballsy it was for her to get in his face, as his oversized chest nearly was busting out of his shirt, while the veins in his abnormally wide, snake-tattooed neck began to throb. To be as fearless in defending her rights in the face of this human grenade that was so clearly about to explode was admirable, especially now that Brian looked back on it, which only reduced him, Chad and all the other onlookers to nothing but an idle audience. Useless. Shameless.

"Goddamn cowards", Brian mumbled to himself, regretting his inactions even more now that he was on the verge of encountering her assailant.

And then he saw movement in the distance. A metal door behind the still closed gate had opened and out walked three men. Brian slowly moved the car across the road to where it was now, roughly fifty feet from the gate. There were no other cars. He wondered just how Randy Scanlon was going to get to wherever he planned to live, and where that was. Would he have the gall to return to Queens, where he had lived prior? His lone sibling was out of state, according to the online papers. Would he move in with his judge father, who may or may not have been the reason why he was getting out so early? *What kind of life does he think he has a right to have?*, Brian angrily asked himself. The men appeared to be engaged in a conversation and were not moving, while Brian continued to ponder how this would go:

If he comes out of the gate, whether he's alone or with a guard, I'll just walk right up to him. I'm not a good enough shooter to try from a distance. I'll just…I'll just walk right up to him and put one in his head. Even if he survives, he won't be able to function. He wouldn't be able to re-marry, re-divorce and kill another ex-wife. Or kill or hurt anyone.

And then he thought about what he had tried to *not* think about, which was anything of value to him that he was leaving behind. He got to spend a last night with his father, and that seemed enough. He had a decent phone chat with his sister, and that seemed enough. He learned something about his mother, which was more than he ever wanted to know. He never called Vanessa back, and since it'd been a while, he assumed she'd forgotten him by now and could live without his friendship. He had nothing to say to his co-workers at Food-on-Feet. Jakween would hopefully forget his last sighting of a shoeless Brian being escorted by police out of the children's playground, but didn't particularly care of what Chad or his family thought, having witnessed the same. Sara was likely dating someone else or maybe even married by now and could care less about Brian. All his old friends were long done with him. Ms. Fochetti had died, and so seemed to represent the utter lawlessness of the world as he had come to know it. He tried. He resented that it took such a horrible criminal act for him to become a more enlightened person, only for him to question just how enlightened he ever became. Was he just a vessel that was recording old adages and proverbs? For all the time given at his job, the hours he never reported, the volunteering, the blood donations, the charity events, the mass visits, confessions, the voluminous readings on spirituality and selflessness, he now knew he just was what he was.

And so why even be unsure of the aftermath of all this? he asked himself. *Why test the outcome? Yeah, I can sit in a cell the rest of my life, but I can also just end it myself. End it for Scanlon and end it for me.*

Yes, he thought. That was what he needed to affirm. He didn't need to take up space any more than Randy Scanlon did.

Suddenly his phone buzzed, as he jumped in his seat. It was the last thing he expected, and he didn't even think to turn off the ringer to avoid even the possibility of a distraction. He reluctantly looked down at the screen to find that it was a number he had never seen, from an unknown source. It wasn't work. It wasn't Kim, his father or even Vanessa. It had to be a telemarketer, or quite possibly the Blood Center reminding him of an upcoming drive he could donate to.

That's fitting, he thought. *You're experiencing your last free minutes, and they call wanting blood.*

Then he looked up, and the three men were approaching the gate. His heart began to race again, as he debated whether to keep the gun in the bag or to put it between his back and his jean belt, like the detectives on television. The men continued their journey towards the gate. Suddenly a cab pulled up. *What the hell?* Brian thought. *They call a cab for them?* If there was no one else to pick them up, there was that option, he now assumed. This was a world unknown to him. But he wouldn't let the surroundings distract him. The cab waited outside the gate, just a few feet from Brian. He then got out of his car, and ducked his head so that the approaching men could not clearly see him. There was a sudden squawk from a crow that landed atop the gate, which appeared to be bleak symbolism for what was to come.

Brian was now shaking, while still holding the backpack. He then quickly put the backpack in the car, closed the door. He then felt behind him and realized he hadn't taken the gun out, so he grabbed the bag, removed the rags and then took out the gun, which he placed behind his back while still holding it.

He waited. The three men were close enough for Brian to notice that two were clearly guards, and the one in the middle appeared to be a prisoner who was about to become a civilian. It was a white man, with a white T-shirt, a tan-colored bomber jacket and jeans.

He appeared to be smiling at something the guard was saying to him, as if they were friends. This infuriated Brian, as he tightened his sweaty grip on the gun. He started to picture the action in his mind, as if a rerun from an existing event. In his mind, it was seamless: The gate would open, the guards would let Scanlon out. Then as he walked towards the cab, Brian would shout "Hey, Randy!" Scanlon would then stop, as Brian would aim with the elegance of a seasoned marksman, before shooting Randy in the forehead.

He waited. As they got closer, Brian attempted to make out the features of the man in the middle. He seemed thin. His hair seemed the same, but with some gray added. A buzzcut, not unlike the cut Scanlon had when Brian had first seen him that evening. They were still approaching, when Brian suddenly had the compulsion to approach the cabbie:

"Excuse me," Brian was halted upon seeing the driver, as it was the same one who brought him to the car rental shop. "Um, I'm sorry, who…who are you here to see?"

The cabbie looked at Brian strangely. "You with the prison?"

Brian paused, "No."

"Didn't I give you a lift earlier?"

Brian paused again, as he looked over at the three approaching men, only now the man in the middle was starting to separate as he was getting close to the gate. "Um, yeah, I guess."

"Are you related?" the cabbie asked.

"To who?" Brian asked.

"To him."

Brian was becoming fidgety, with the gun now nestled between his back and belt buckle, as he looked over at the approaching man. *Is it him?* he wondered. *He's so thin.* Brian anxiously turned back to the driver. "Look, do you know who he is? The prisoner?"

"No," he replied. "They don't give us names. They always do this, when someone doesn't have a ride. What, are *you* pickin' him up?"

"Fuck it," Brian replied, then stormed back to his car, as it was a better angle to see the man who was about to enter through the opening gate, which slid open so slowly, it was as if to give Brian time to reconsider. *You sonofabitch! No more. No more. This is the one thing I can do. The one Goddamn thing, and I'm doing it, you piece of shit. This is the one damn thing!*

The gate opened, and out he came – only Brian still wasn't sure. He was so much thinner, if it was him. But it couldn't be. The Randy Scanlon he remembered was built like a bull without horns. Barrel-chested, arms that popped like veined balloons, his neck as wide as a tree trunk… The frail, thin man that ambled out couldn't be the same. He began to approach the cab, as Brian stood confused. *Is that him?* he asked, with urgency. The man seemed weak, like he could barely open a can of Coke let alone beat a woman to death. He walked slowly, as if getting used to walking as a civilian. His pale skin accentuated his seeming lack of strength.

"Sir?!" called one of the guards. The man turned to see Brian standing there, staring at him. Suddenly, the man stopped, looked at him as if he knew Brian would be his messenger of death. He stood still, as if to brace himself for what was to come, and yet he seemed so willing – not fearful, but desiring of his own end. Brian then looked at his neck, and there was the snake tattoo. It was him, but a different him. A shell of himself.

"Sir?!" the guard called out again, as they both came through the gates and approached Brian, as Randy Scanlon stood before the waiting cab. To the guards, it was clear from how Brian and Randy were standing apart from each other that this was not intended as any sort of joy-filled reunion. "Are you here for a reason, sir?" the guard asked firmly, not unlike the policeman asked him at the children's playground. Brian continued to look at Randy, whose eyes still appeared to predict his own death. But the guards now stood between them. "Sir, you can't be here. Are you family?"

The other guard could then be heard asking, "Randy, is he family?"

Randy then looked at the guard, aware that he was still alive, then shook his head, "I've never… No," he said, softly.

Brian kept his eyes on Randy, but the rage had dissipated. It was hard to remain committed to wanting to end the life of someone who seemed so feeble. Was it the year and a half of not taking steroids that made him so thin? Was he ill? He didn't know. He still hated this man. That much was still possible. But he just couldn't kill him.

The guard briskly escorted Randy to the back door of the cab, as the other guard advised Brian, "Don't do something foolish, sir," as the guard moved his hand to his holster.

Brian was struck by this. While he hadn't revealed the gun to them, the guards could sense the potential of their encounter. They had probably seen it before.

"I'll go," Brian managed, but it was more directed at the air and from his own disappointment and confusion than influenced by the guard. The cab sped off, and Brian watched the car fade uphill into the horizon. He stood there for what seemed like minutes; still, and frozen in thought – before the squawk of the returning crow thrust him out of his numbed state. He looked to see that the gate was closed, and the guards were gone. A half-hour had elapsed, yet he didn't feel it.

It was as if nothing had happened.

Twenty

—

After standing alone at the gate of Branding Correctional Facility for what seemed like a lifetime, under the only eyes of a black crow atop the closed prison gate, he brought the car back to the rental shop. In order to avoid the possibility of seeing the same cabbie again, he decided to take the 30 minute walk to the train station. On the ride back, he was numb. Still with his backpack, wherein resided the loaded .38, he didn't even consider getting off in Crawberry to somehow return it to his father. He could barely fathom getting off at Penn Station in the city, as it appeared to him that there was no real destination for him. He knew very little about what his future held, having been so determined to end Randy Scanlon's life. Now that he had, in essence, allowed him to live, it called into question how Brian was to proceed with his own life. He couldn't think of going back to Food-on-Feet much more than he could think of returning to his apartment, which he was so certain that he wouldn't see again. What was there to him now was what he remembered from one of his many spiritual readings which spoke of the utter needlessness of things; possessions aren't even really possessions, when you consider that we all die. And in our death, the things we possessed and were so precious about become simply things to be tossed into the trash or taken by someone else. Everything in life was dispensable. The question for Brian, though, was if anything in his possession was ever worth anything, even to him.

His apartment had become a storage room, basically. Square footage containing some furniture pieces, appliances, books and DVDs he had accumulated, all with the intent of improving himself and keeping his shame at bay. As he passed by the same houses he had passed by just a day before, he felt that maybe the gun might still come in handy. What was there to live for? He thought of Jeff Gammon, in particular, and how distant all his philosophies seemed to him now. He didn't even think about the unproven sexual abuse accusations which someday might come to fruition. Now he just saw him as any salesman, not unlike whatever telemarketing call he may have received as he was waiting outside the prison. Perhaps Gammon did indeed seek to have a more authentic and altruistic life and his giving away a large portion of his wealth was symbolic of his commitment to the cause he so passionately preached. But it now appeared to Brian that it didn't matter what Gammon had. He was likely a millionaire again anyway, just by the sales of his books and how much he would get to speak. And even if that money was largely given back to charitable foundations, Gammon was still just a person, in the end. He didn't originate anything that he said, but admittedly borrowed and infused his speeches from any in a myriad of other philosophers and spiritualists. They all were the same. Just like Father Devon. He took the words of the Bible and other sources, and was merely a vessel to give false comfort to those who felt they needed it.

Brian knew now, without question, that he was alone in the world and, in the end, perhaps his own life's journey was meant to come to that very conclusion.

He looked down at his phone and noticed the recent voicemail message. It could not have felt more useless to him to check it, as he was all but certain that it was some sort of solicitation or possibly a notification that he had forgotten to pay a utility bill:

"Uh, yeah, 'dis is Lou from Ladder 17 at East 143rd. You had... I think you're the guy. You came in askin' about a cat 'dat was rescued in a recent fire. It turns out one of our guys here wanted to take it in, but 'dey got a newborn'n she was havin' allergic reactions'n this'n that... Anyway, I think you came in and asked about it, so right now he's at the firehouse. If you... I don't know if you want 'im. He's not in great shape, but he's a toughy. I forget the name you said he had.

We been callin' 'im Rocky, 'cause he's a tough little sonofabitch, but maybe you... Anyway, you can call or come by, if you'd like to adopt 'im. He needs kinda' special care, jus' so you know. His fur's all fucked up...messed up, sorry, n'matted, but...he's alive, so... There ya' go."

Brian could barely believe his ears. Of all the calls he thought he would receive, hearing from the grumpy Lou at Ladder 17 regarding the whereabouts of Socrates was probably the furthest from his mind. When he recalled coming into the firehouse and leaving his information a couple of weeks ago, he was all but certain he would never hear anything and had resigned that Socrates' fate would not be dissimilar to Robert's, the caller at the suicide hotline; he would never know for sure, but felt strongly that it would be a sad outcome. And yet, Socrates was alive. He knew this now, and yet he was the only one who knew that Socrates was even called Socrates. At the very least, that information needed to be shared. Ms. Fochetti did name him, after all. His name deserved to be preserved.

He dialed:

"Ladder 17. Martelli," he barked.

"Uh, yeah...I'm... This is... Is this Lou?"

"No, this is Vince. Who's this?" the bass-voiced fireman responded, sounding no less than 6'2".

"This is Brian. He... Lou called me about the cat, Socra... *Rocky* you guys call him?"

"Oh, yeah. You pickin' 'im up?" Vic seemed to assume more than ask.

"Uh, no, I... I just wanted to let you know that I know his name."

"Know his what?"

"His name. It's *Socrates*. So...call him that, please."

"How d'you know?"

Brian paused, "I was friends with the woman who named him. The one who died in the fire."

"You don't want 'im?" Vince asked, as if disappointed.

Brian looked out the window, as the train was now just minutes from the city. He couldn't begin to explain why. "It's not that I don't. It's just, I'm... My apartment... I can't have cats, and I'm allergic, and...I have a baby and..." Brian felt strangely compelled to list excuses, which were, chronologically, not quite true, true and then utterly absurd. He wasn't sure that he couldn't have pets, though he *was*, in fact, allergic,...*but a baby?*

"So, no," Vince confirmed, as if Brian had revealed more than enough.

The abruptness took Brian back. Could he tell this stranger that he couldn't bring a cat home for the main reason that he may very well decide to blow his brains out that evening and, therefore, the cat would only be abandoned again?

He paused, then swallowed. "No, I'm sorry."

"Hey, we jus' needed to know. We can't keep 'em here, is all."

"You can't?"

"No, we can't keep a three-legged cat. The thing could get hurt. Plus we already got a cat here who keeps the mice out, Turbo, and he's pretty territorial. So that's not an option. Alright, so, we'll have to figure somethin' out."

Brian hoped at the very least that he could stay at the firehouse and imagined that the crew would look at Socrates as a sort of symbol of strength and valor, or some such thing. "Like what?"

"Probably a shelter. Maybe one of the other guys can take 'em, but I doubt it. Socra*what*, y'said?"

"*Socrates*," Brian corrected.

"Alright, well, I guess that's it, unless you have any suggestions."

"Well, I… I don't know what… I just don't want him to die, y'know?"

There was an odd pause from the otherwise abrupt fireman. "You sure you can't take 'im, dude?"

Brian paused again, then sadly emitted "No,…sorry. Thank you." He clicked off, stared at his phone and wondered why that had occurred. Why should that have been brought to his attention, that Socrates would be saved only to most likely end up in a shelter anyway, where the will of this creature could only weaken as a result of all it had been through, leading to his eventual, lonely death. Wasn't it enough that Brian was just accepting this of himself? That he was alone, and would die alone. And why not cease prolonging this existence that seemed to be nothing but a vaporous pursuit?

Why this complication?, he thought, resentfully,…as the train pulled into Penn Station.

Twenty One

He stood in the center of Penn Station. The vastness of the complex made Brian feel even more inconsequential, as the early afternoon rush encircled him. This was the world. People in motion, going somewhere with seeming determination. And there he was, dead center, with nowhere to go. An apartment, but not a home. A way station, at best. What was keeping him here? He could pull out the gun now and end it – and that would at least let some people know that he was ever here.   He'd be in the news for ten minutes before something more tragic would usurp it. But that would be wrong, too, he thought. The last thing he wanted was to dramatize his death and traumatize others. It wasn't about imposing shock on strangers. It was about his pathetic self. It was solely to spare himself living with such internal pain. If he had shot Randy Scanlon, he'd be in custody right now, and the rest of his story would be so easily written. He wouldn't have to think. He would just exist in a cell.

Perhaps help tutor prisoners or something, but it would be easier than navigating through this vortex of so-called freedom.

As he looked at the perpetually moving commuters, he affirmed that the only thing that justified any of their efforts to get to wherever they were going was that they believed that someone somewhere cared for them. Needed them. He could only conclude that no one needed him, as he started to make his way out of the station, before passing a mural. He thought nothing of its enormity and its blaringly bright colors, until he caught sight of a small, primping cat in the corner of it, as if inserted as an afterthought by the artist.

Brian stopped and became fixated on it, as the bodies passed him. He reached his hand out and touched the painted cat. He then realized something.

"Vince said you didn't want 'im," quipped Lou, who stood at the open garage door to the firehouse, again with a cigarette and Diet Coke.

"I know. I wasn't sure. But…I'll take 'im," Brian said with trepidation. After all, he wasn't aware what Socrates' condition actually was. He could end up looking like some sort of Frankenstein, re-assembled from various sources, and all of it done haphazardly. Lou walked him to the lounge area where a few of his brethren loafed with plates of freshly made lasagna. Brian saw that they had a dining table adjacent to them, and was surprised to see the men eating on TV trays or even with plates on their laps. But he soon discovered why they were there. There in the center of the couch was this matted brown, tan and white mass, its eyes green but slightly grayed over. A clipped left ear. He was sitting up, his one hind leg folded under him, as his left front leg braced himself against a fireman's plate as he feebly licked a portion of marinara sauce from it. They laughed with endearment at the cat's apparent love for Italian cuisine.

"I told you he'd like my sauce, assholes!" barked Lou, who was apparently responsible for the afternoon meal.

The firemen guffawed, not yet catching sight of Brian standing behind.

Lou followed, "So this guy's takin' Rocky."

Suddenly the laughter stopped, and all the men looked at Brian standing there warily with his backpack. It was clear that they were sizing him up to see if he was worthy of being the cat's caretaker.

"Hi," Brian managed. But he just as quickly tuned them out and focused on Socrates, who now looked at Brian. Brian did not think Socrates would recognize him, especially having only ever been visible in spurts within Ms. Fochetti's dimly lit apartment. However, it also crossed his mind that the cat may *indeed* recognize him and even possibly despise him, recalling him as the strange sneezing man who continually placed meals on his tail. Before Brian knew it, he was closer to the couch where Socrates still sat upright. He could assess the damage clearly. He had been cleaned up, but he had various bald patches along his body. His tail appeared to have been singed at the end. He was reluctant to touch him, first out of a lack of familiarity with handling cats and also because he assumed the cat would have various sensitivities, given all that it had been through.

"Well, let's get ya' ready for your new home, Rocky," said one of the men, who rose to get a small carrying cage.

"*Socrates*," Brian mumbled, as he looked at him.

"What?" another crew man asked.

"His name is Socrates. That's what his original owner named him. Like the Greek philosopher," Brian said, almost subconsciously.

The man put the small cage on the coffee table, as another man gently picked up Socrates and placed him carefully inside. The large man with fingers the size of bratwursts closed the cage door with unusual delicacy, as he then turned the cage to face Brian, who looked down at it awkwardly.

"He's all yours," the man followed.

"You want some lasagna?" asked Lou.

Brian was surprised by the offer. "Oh, that's ok, thanks."

"Not for you. For the cat. He likes it."

The men laughed, as Brian looked back at Socrates in the cage, then back at Lou. "Uh, sure. Thanks."

Lou went off to the nearby kitchen, as Brian kneeled down to look at Socrates through the cage door. He did not have any particular expression. He appeared too fatigued to complain that Brian had interrupted his meal. For that matter, he appeared to be simply going with the flow of his recently imposed vagabond existence. He was likely resigned to the fact that a nomadic life was to be expected, even if he still couldn't process that Ms. Fochetti had died and that his home was no more. Life had begun for him similarly and, perhaps, it would end the same.

"Here ya' go," Lou handed Brian a large, sealed plastic container wherein a larger than expected piece of lasagna with extra sauce resided.

Brian looked at Lou, "Thank you." He then looked at the men, who were now in discussion about something unrelated, laughing and eating. It helped that he and the cat were no longer the focus, as he picked up the cage…and left.

***

It was ironic, to say the least. Forty-eight hours prior, he was certain that he would never be returning to the city. That he would be arrested or shot down. Yet now, he was in a cab heading to Queens with lasagna, his father's gun and a three-legged cat. *What a world,* he thought, as they headed over the Bronx-Queens Expressway. Socrates uttered not a sound the entire trip, as Brian occasionally peaked in to make sure he was still breathing. *This is all too much for him,* he thought. *What if I get him home and he just dies in front of me?* He wondered why he was going through all this, especially when he was so determined to faze himself out – if not that day, then soon, because he just didn't see things improving. But it was like something was taking him over, and his actions belied his instincts to let things run their proper course. Socrates was a battered cat who already was somewhat of a miracle with how he had survived thus far. Why test the poor thing further with a commute to Queens? And what if Brian's dander allergies rendered the situation impossible? He could barely afford medications with what he made at Food-on-Feet. And who knows if he even had a job anymore? And if he even wanted it now.

Death still seemed the best option.

He picked up a few cans of cheap cat food from the local bodega before they headed up to his apartment. It was weird returning. He almost expected that his stuff would be gone, even though he was only away for a day. A lifetime appeared to have elapsed in this trip, and now he was returning and it seemed so strange, like fate was weirdly altered. *What did it all mean to go through all that? To find out what I did? To come back with...?* He stared at his apartment which, even though it had gone untouched since his departure, felt empty to him. It took him a few minutes before a cantankerous "Myooooww!" emanated from the cage he was still holding.

"Oh, shoot…" He quickly placed the cage onto the floor and opened it. Socrates, to his surprise, exercised the exact right time to speak, as if to announce that he was ready to peruse his new surroundings. Out he limped, slowly, with his three legs, grayed over green eyes, matted hair and bald patches. He looked around and moved towards the large window which observed 34th Ave. Brian then delicately walked to the kitchen, as Socrates remained on the floor. The sun shone on the cat as if it were welcoming him to Heaven. Brian came back with a small plate and placed it delicately in front of Socrates, who smelled it thoroughly before carefully sampling. Brian watched awkwardly, afraid to move too far away or too close. Since he was a relatively small cat, Brian feared accidentally stepping on him. *Wouldn't that be an end?* he thought. He then realized he still had the lasagna from the firehouse. It didn't seem to be the healthiest thing to give a cat, but he *did* appear to like the sauce. So Brian brought a small plate of it and set it alongside the plate of cat food, then followed that with a small cup of water - then followed that with a small cup of milk. He felt he may have been overcompensating with such a vast buffet, but wanted to cover all the bases of the cat's possible tastes. By tomorrow, he figured he would bring him to a vet and make sure if he needed any medications. *Who knows what that'll cost*, he pondered, knowing his bank account had barely enough to cover the next month's rent.

He went to get his backpack, which he hesitantly looked inside. The gun remained, wrapped in his father's shoe rags. He wondered what he should do with it, before realizing it'd be best atop his own closet shelf.

He came back to the living room and observed Socrates in front of his feast. He even found himself momentarily grinning at how the cat went from plate to bowl, though not without judgement: a bit of the cat food, a bit of the sauce, a sip of water, then a sip of milk – then repeat. *This can't be good for him*, Brian thought, *but why the hell not?*

He soon found himself sitting on the floor, about three feet from where Socrates continued to indulge. Brian's cheeks felt strained, since the very slight smile that the cat managed to inadvertently generate from him was the first time he had smiled in days. His face having become a mask of pensiveness. Joylessness. Sadness. Suddenly, all the sources of it came back to him, and he would reveal what he had not been able to tell anyone before:

"Boy, didn't you draw the short straw," he weakly snickered. "From a dumpster to here. I wish I could say you're better off here, but..." Brian watched Socrates lap up the bit of milk in the cup, before he turned to the window. "This is a lawless world, I'll tell ya'. People kill others, and then they just walk. An animal can be thrown in the trash. And then there's…there's people who just watch it all and do nothing." Brian found himself speaking as if the deepest recesses of his soul were expelling a raw truth without accompaniment of his mind, as his voice began to tremble… "And you know what? I'm the worst of them. I know this now. I've…I've tried to hide what I did, or didn't do. I've tried to…to mask it all. But I've just…I've been kidding myself," and then he started to cry. "I'm the worst of them, Socrates. I'm…I'm…I'm the worst of them all…" Brian broke down, sobbing, howling as if an injured animal in the mountains who had no thoughts of embarrassment. The façade was gone. There was no hiding anymore. Everything was out and being screamed at the sky. This was all that he could do. His tears continued to flow out of his eyes, as he sat on the floor, before he heard a piercing "Myow…!" which resonated as nothing less than an exclamatory demand.

Brian looked down within his lap and, to his surprise, he saw Socrates, nestled within his entwined legs, looking up, while trying to catch the tear drops that were raining onto him with his tongue. Brian could not help but laugh at the sight, before he eventually stopped crying and just watched the cat lick the tears that had fallen onto his paws and chest.

He watched him for several minutes, before realizing that the cat's timing was not arbitrary. It was communicating something as only a cat could. There was no artifice to it. There was no bumper sticker phrases or biblical quotes. There was no sappy violin underscoring, like in the movies. He knew that Socrates was simply telling him to shut up. Brian had given him a home, and the cat was fine with it. In the moment, it appeared to be the only advice that Brian needed.

They remained sitting before the window, with the afternoon sun coming in. Eventually, it dawned on Brian that in the whole time that he had been in the cat's presence, he hadn't sneezed once or experienced any allergic reaction. He thought that somehow the fire or smoke may have managed to conveniently remove the dander. Or perhaps he had somehow developed an immunity. It was all a mystery.

His legs were beginning to cramp in their folded position, but he did not want to disturb how comfortable Socrates seemed. So he just sat there and endured. Eventually, he knew he'd get up.

And when he did, maybe he'd call Vanessa.

***

Daniel Damiano is an Award-winning Playwright, Actor, Screenwriter, Poet and Novelist based in Brooklyn, NY. His plays have been performed throughout many areas of the U.S., as well as London, England and Sydney & Melbourne, Australia. He has been the recipient of the Christopher Brian Wolk Award for Playwriting, as well as a nominee for the Pushcart Poetry Prize and a Finalist for the Arts & Letters Prize for Drama. Among his published work is his acclaimed play, DAY OF THE DOG (Broadway Play Publishing), his debut novel, THE WOMAN IN THE SUN HAT *(2021 Seattle Book Review Recommendation),* his debut poetry book 104 DAYS OF THE PANDEMIC and his second novel, GRAPHIC NATURE (all published by fandango 4 Art House). In 2024, Bottlecap Press published his second book of poetry, THE CONCRETE JUNGLE AND THE SURROUNDING AREAS. ADVICE FROM A CAT is his third novel.